THE MONDAY
SHEEPDOG

By the same author

The Dingo Summer
If Wishes Were Horses

THE MONDAY SHEEPDOG

IVY · BAKER

ANGUS
& ROBERTSON
PUBLISHERS

*Creative writing programme assisted by
the Literature Board of the Australia Council,
the Federal Government's arts funding and
advisory body.*

ANGUS & ROBERTSON PUBLISHERS

**Unit 4, Eden Park, 31 Waterloo Road,
North Ryde, NSW, Australia 2113, and
16 Golden Square, London W1R 4BN,
United Kingdom**

*This book is copyright.
Apart from any fair dealing for the
purposes of private study, research,
criticism or review, as permitted
under the Copyright Act, no part may
be reproduced by any process without
written permission. Inquiries should
be addressed to the publishers.*

*First published in Australia
by Angus & Robertson Publishers in 1987
First published in the United Kingdom
by Angus & Robertson UK in 1987*

© *Copyright Ivy Baker, 1987*

ISBN 0 207 15587 9

*Typeset in 12/13 Plantin
Printed in Australia*

For Saul and Sophie

Contents

C r i s i s !

Today was the last day of the school holidays. Ben had finished his lunch, so now he decided that he would climb Mount Everest.

It was not the real Mount Everest, of course. Around their homestead the land was level, but just before their property ended, a small hill bulged up like an enormous grass-covered tooth; a geological joke, his grandfather said. It had been his grandfather who had named it Mount Everest when he had lived on the farm years before.

Ben could almost remember when Mount Everest had been too steep for him to climb, and he could vaguely recall that his grandfather used to carry him at least halfway up the hill himself; nowadays he could walk all the way to the top quite easily, without stopping. Last Sunday, when his grandfather had visited them, he had stood watching while Ben had shown him how fast he could get up to the top of the hill and back.

'Well done, Ben,' he said when Ben returned, puffing only a little.

'Aren't you coming up, too?' Ben asked.

'Not this time, Ben.'

As they strolled back to the farm together that afternoon, it had seemed to Ben that his grandfather walked more slowly than usual, and stopped more often to rest. I suppose that he's getting old, Ben thought uncomfortably, and the idea was so upsetting that he found it difficult to go out to say goodbye when his grandfather got into his car to drive back to the city.

Today, Ben climbed Mount Everest briskly. He was halfway up the steep slope when he heard the blare of a horn. It was the tourist coach making its daily run in to the Coonara Hotel, taking the tourists there for lunch because the township of Coonara was a showpiece, with many of its pioneers' buildings still intact. The coach driver always sounded the horn before turning the sharp corner at the foot of Mount Everest. Ben paused to wave, as he normally did, and he saw a couple of handkerchiefs flutter in response from the smudges at the windows.

He reached the top and sat down on the grass with his back to the farmhouse, looking towards Coonara. He could not see the town, but he could watch the metalled road below, twining like a dark grey ribbon around the hills. It uncoiled for a brief, straight run along the front of their property until the road reached the base of Mount Everest just below him. There, it swivelled around in a hairpin bend before it began to curl across the mountains again — but out of sight now — on its way across to the main highway.

The hills to the north were flecked with cattle, for this was dairy country. McGlosker was the only one amongst their neighbours who kept sheep. From where he sat on Mount Everest, Ben could see some of those sheep sprinkled here and there like coconut on the southern hills. The stubborn river red gums still clung grimly to the rises over there, their muscular trunks slanted against the wind, their unkempt branches straggling. No trees grew on Mount Everest, only thick native grasses like the tufted kangaroo grass; and in the spring, clumps of wildflowers like the vivid yellow paper-daisies or the misty-mauve sun orchids.

Usually Mount Everest was a quiet place, but today the screech of an electric saw, stopping and starting, reminded Ben that his father was cutting timber for a new fence. It was to be erected around the fowlhouse, to keep out the foxes. He had not wanted Ben to help.

'No,' he said. 'It's the last day of your holidays. Go along now, and enjoy yourself.'

Ben had nothing left to do. He had prepared for everything. His bag was already packed. He had pumped up the tyres on his bike, and he knew precisely how long it would take him to ride down to the bus stop, because he had timed it. He knew exactly where to push his bike in amongst the bushes there, so that it could not be seen from the road. None of the local folk would touch the bike, but his father had warned him that strangers might, so that he must conceal it. Ben had also set his alarm clock for the morning. Even though his parents always rose early, because this was a dairy farm where cows had to be milked twice each day, and although he knew that his mother would come and wake him if he overslept, Ben felt that he should be able to get up in time now, without her help.

The sound of the saw had stopped. It seemed to have left a gap in the air that waited to be filled. Ben lay back on the grass and gazed up at the blue sky above him. Plump white clouds hovered over the river, but further to the west they dangled, like frayed and stringy washing, and he observed them gloomily. I suppose it'll rain tomorrow, he thought. But it won't matter, because I'm ready for that, too. I've packed a raincoat. I haven't forgotten a thing. Not a thing. I'm ready for anything.

This year – tomorrow – he was starting high school. Before, he had merely cycled down to the local Coonara school each day, but now, since there was no high school at Coonara, he would have to catch the school bus and

3

travel about fifty kilometres to the high school. He had to leave home earlier, but so did all the other kids in his class. It would be fun. And he had made quite sure that he would not miss the school bus.

He heard the strain of an engine toiling around one of the hills in the distance and he sat up, listening. He saw the sun flash on the windscreen of a van, and he heard the screeches of crimson rosellas that had been startled into the air and now circled like a small squadron, waiting for the van to pass. If it's a local driver, Ben thought, he'll know that he has to slow down for the hairpin bend down below Mount Everest, here. It could be more fun to watch if it was a stranger driving, for even though the road signs clearly said "Slow Down" and "Dangerous Bend", many drivers ignored them and took the corner too fast.

It swirled down out of the hills, a truck of medium size with a tarpaulin tied over a high load. It accelerated as soon as it reached the straight stretch of road in front of the farm, and Ben whistled softly to himself at its speed. The tarpaulin was loose, flapping in and out at the sides, like lungs bursting to maintain the pace that the driver had set. Ben waited for some reaction as the truck approached the road signs below, but the driver seemed to ignore them, and was almost too late braking for the corner. The scream of his brakes flared through the air as he swerved, braked at last, but too quickly, then skidded around.

Ben was on his feet, waving and whistling. In that first moment of turning, the tarpaulin at the back of the truck tore open, and as the driver wrestled the vehicle back on to the road, a large crate flew off, half bounced, half slid across the road, and disappeared into the bushes.

Ben whistled his loudest. He waved frantically to catch the driver's eye, and he was almost sure that he saw the driver's hand go up to acknowledge him.

'You've dropped something!' Ben shouted. 'Stop! Stop!'

He pointed back along the road and shouted, then whistled again, as loudly as he could. But the truck sped on, its tarpaulin cover still hanging open. Within another minute it had disappeared around the final bend, and Ben could hear the driver changing gears halfway up the next hill. Ben stood, disgusted, wondering what he should do next. He must have heard me whistling, he thought; he must have. At school Miss Cameron had often complained that his whistle was deafening, and that it was the noisiest that she'd ever heard. And surely the driver didn't think that he'd been jumping up and down like that, and waving, all for nothing?

Ben grinned, remembering the skid. I bet he got a fright then. It served him right, tearing along like that. He'll be halfway to Jindagery by now, at the rate that he was going. Ben wished that the rosellas would settle down again, now that the truck had gone, and stop shredding the air with their metallic calls.

Suddenly, he realised that it was not just the birds that he could hear. His mother was calling him, yet it didn't sound like her voice at all; it was different somehow. Was she screaming? His blood ran cold, and he plunged down Mount Everest as fast as he could run.

She was standing up by the home paddock fence, and she began to shout at him as he ran, 'Hurry, Ben! Hurry!', so that by the time he was close enough to ask her what was wrong and why she looked so frightened, he was out of breath. He climbed over the gate, not pausing to untie it, and stood beside her.

'What is it, Mum? What's happened?' he managed to gasp.

She was close to tears, he could tell, and he could

5

see her throat wobble a bit as she made a tremendous effort to speak. Her face was an odd, chalky colour. He asked again, urgently.

'What's wrong?'

'Your father. He's had an accident.'

Ben felt his heart jump. His mother held out her hand to him aimlessly, as though she was lost, and he grabbed it, but he grew even more frightened then because it felt so cold. He heard her take a deep breath.

'He's cut his hand with the saw. You know he was building the fence. He's in the kitchen, waiting. I'm going to drive him in to the Coonara Hospital straight away. I've rung them, and they're waiting for us. Ben, do you think that you can manage here till we get back?'

Ben did not stop to think what 'manage' might mean; he had never seen his mother look so upset, so he would have said 'yes' to anything. She hardly waited to catch his nod as she turned to half run, half walk back to the farmhouse. Ben hurried beside her.

'It's his hand, you said, Mum?'

'I've bandaged it as well as I could, but it looked dreadful, and I know it'll have to be stitched. Ben, I've been trying to think—the milking has to be done this evening, but the Carters will help you with that, so give them a ring and tell them what's happened. Their number's in the little green notebook beside the phone. And I'll ring you just as soon as I can, from the hospital. Do you think you'll be all right?'

Ben could see that she was trying to tick things off in her mind, but her concentration was focused on his father. When they arrived back at the house she tried three times to open the back door, but she seemed to have forgotten that the latch was on the opposite side, so that finally Ben had to reach across and open it for her.

His father was sitting very still and straight with

6

his back to them and his arm flat on the kitchen table. He did not turn around when they came in, and Ben's gaze riveted on the white bandages, noting the blood staining through.

'Dad?' Ben wanted to ask his father if he felt all right, but he seemed to have lost his voice. His father heard him though, and turned around.

'Don't worry, Ben. I'll be all right,' he said, each word very slow and alarmingly distinct. 'Mum's taking me in to the hospital.'

His mother had gone inside; now she returned with her handbag in one hand and the car keys in the other.

'I'll bring the car around to the front,' she told Ben. 'Will you see if you can help him outside?'

Ben heard her start the car, revving it more than usual. He moved closer as his father stood, then he took some of his father's weight as, together, they moved rather shakily to the front door.

'Get hold of the Carters, Ben,' his father told him, repeating what his mother had said earlier. 'Ring them as soon as we've gone. Bill Carter will give you a hand with the milking until I get back.'

His voice trailed away, and he gripped Ben's shoulder very hard. After a long pause his hand loosened and they moved out on to the verandah. Ben's mother hurried to open the car door.

'Sit here in the back,' she urged. 'You'll have more room there, and you can lie back. You'll be more comfortable. There! A pillow!' She signalled Ben with her eyes, and he ran inside for one. As he tried to wedge it behind his father's back his mother revved the motor and looked distractedly across at Ben.

'Don't forget,' she told him. 'Ring the Carters. You'd better do that straight away, so that they can arrange to come over later and help you.' She leaned over to kiss him goodbye. 'I'll ring you and tell you how things

7

are going, just as soon as I can.'

'Sure,' Ben said. 'Look, don't worry about a thing. Hey! Just wait a minute.' He shut the rear door of the car, then got in beside his mother. 'I'll come up to the front with you, so that you won't have to get out to open the gate.'

They bounced too fast over the cattlegrid. His father groaned, and Ben heard his mother catch her breath.

'Oh, I'm so sorry. I forgot. I'll try to watch out for the bumps. We can make up time on the road.'

As soon as they reached the gate Ben jumped out and swung it open as quickly as he could. His mother drove through on to the road, gave him a sketchy wave, then changed gears and gathered speed as they headed in the direction of Coonara. Ben watched until they were well out of sight, then he pulled the gate shut and secured it firmly as he had always been taught; for if gates were left open, you lost valuable stock. Everything around the farm had become abnormally quiet and still in the afternoon sun, and he walked slowly back along the drive to the house, his boots chipping and crunching the gravel as he went.

Alone
on the farm

As soon as Ben re-entered the house he went straight to the telephone. He must ring the Carters to ask them to come over and help him with the evening milking; they lived on the neighbouring farm and had a dairy herd. He found their number, dialled it, and waited, hearing it ring and ring. No one answered. They might be out in the milking sheds, or in the paddocks, he thought as he hung up. He moved around the room for a few minutes, uncertain whether to ring again or not, then he went back and stood looking down at the telephone. Well, perhaps he had dialled wrongly; he would try once more. The phone rang while Ben waited anxiously. He was about to hang up the receiver again when there was a sudden gap in the ringing, and after a pause someone spoke.

'Hello!'

It was too low and husky a voice to be Mrs Carter's, and Ben wondered if he should speak, or simply hang up and try a third time.

'Could I speak to Mrs Carter, please?' he asked, instead.

'Yes, speaking. Who's that?'

'It's Ben, Mrs Carter,' he said. 'Mum told me—'

'Oh, it's you, Ben,' she interrupted. 'I'm sorry, but I can hardly hear you. Bill and I are both down with a virus. I wasn't going to answer the phone at all, but then I thought it might be an emergency.' She broke off, coughing, then resumed even more huskily. 'Ben, will you tell your mother that I won't be able to go to that meeting with her tomorrow? I suppose that's why you're ringing—' Her voice wavered, and she coughed again. 'I'll have to go, Ben,' she said at last, in a near whisper. 'And tell your mother that I'm sorry. 'Bye.'

Ben was left staring at the silent phone. What was he to do now? Was there anyone else he could call? He racked his brains, but no other name came conveniently to mind. Whenever small emergencies had arisen in the past, Mr Carter had helped them; and Ben could remember his father working at the Carters' farm when things had gone wrong for them. He went outside, still wondering what he should do, and looked across to the paddocks where the cows were grazing quietly. He could distinguish Bossy and Star in one group, and his heart sank. Somehow, he had to milk the cows. Even Bossy and Star.

Since it was now late summer, their herd was smaller. Some of the cows had already been dried off, and turned out into the top paddock for a few months; but more than a hundred cows still remained as the milking herd. The longer Ben thought about the job that he would have to do, the harder it seemed. Was there no one else that he could ring? His grandfather? But he lived so far away that he would take hours to come; anyway, Ben remembered how tired he had appeared to be, the last time that he had visited them.

Then he thought about McGlosker, and his spirits lifted. Even though McGlosker was really a sheep man, Ben was sure that he would help. He returned to the phone. This time, although he waited while the phone rang and rang, no one answered, and at last he had to hang up. Reluctantly, he went outside at last and down to the milking sheds.

He checked all the machinery there very carefully, and was glad that it looked to be in working order; the hoses were all firmly attached and when he turned the taps on to test them, water gushed out of each one. He switched on the electricity next, and walked along checking each of the suction cups. They were all working well. After that, he moved into the small adjoining shed, where a large, stainless steel vat took up most of the space. He checked the temperature gauge on the side of the vat, noting with relief that the cooling system was operating correctly. It was all very well to do all this checking, but he did not know what he would do if he found anything wrong.

By tomorrow, the vat should be full and the milk tanker would come, pump the milk out and take it down to the butter factory in Coonara. The vat would be full if he could manage to do the milking.

Ben had often helped his father with the milking, especially during the school holidays. Together, they could finish the work in an hour or so. He knew that he would take much longer on his own, so he decided that he would start a little earlier, although a quick glance at his watch warned him that he would be earlier by only twenty minutes, even if he started immediately. Wherever had all that time gone? And the weather was changing; those grey clouds that he had observed from Mount Everest earlier, low down on the horizon, were now almost overhead. It was colder too. Suddenly he felt hungry, and he wondered if he would be able to find any food later for his dinner.

His first job would be to drive the cows up from the south paddocks, along the race which was a grassed walkway, and into the holding yard. From there, he could transfer eight cows at a time into the milking shed. It would be slow, but it was the only course that he could think of. Rounding up the cows would take longer too, because his father always rode down to get them on his motorcycle, whereas Ben would have to walk. He ran most of the way.

The majority of their herd were Friesians, large black cows with white markings. A small proportion of the herd were Jerseys, fawn-coloured and a little smaller than the Friesians, and usually very gentle and tractable animals. Bossy was a Friesian, almost entirely black with only a narrow splash of white down one side. Star was a Jersey, but not the usual obedient Jersey. Star had been the leader of the herd until a few months ago, when Ben's father had brought Bossy home from the market. Ever since then, the two cows had been waging a private war for the leadership. Even Ben's placid father became exasperated with Bossy and Star at times; but they were the most valuable cows in the herd.

'Ah well,' his father said. 'Every herd has its Bossy. And every herd must have its leader; Bossy and Star will sort it out between them.'

Creatures of habit, the cows were already collecting together at the bottom of the race when Ben reached them, with Bossy and Star at their head. Ben raced around behind the rest, whistling and shouting to urge them on. Now that they had begun to plod up to the sheds, they all seemed willing enough to continue in the right direction. Even Bossy and Star. Ben, walking close behind the herd, could hardly believe his luck.

But the cows were more than halfway up to the holding yard before Ben remembered that he had forgotten to open the gate at the top of the race to let them through. They would mill around there, and perhaps break down the fence. He stood aghast, wondering what he could do, for the cows were so tightly bunched in front of him that he could not slip through to run ahead of them. He had no choice but to try to reach the gate before them, by dashing back, and around the other way.

He turned and ran down to the bottom of the race, crossed into the south paddock and scrambled over two fences. He reached the gate, panting and exhausted, but at least before the cows arrived there. He dragged the gate open and the cows ambled past him, crowding the holding yard. He could see Bossy in the front; but Star had miscalculated her late run to cut Bossy from the lead, so that she was now jammed near the fence, caught between two large Friesians. Ben was not sorry; this way, he could deal with each cow in a separate group. The animals were as familiar with the milking procedure as Ben was, and Bossy had already taken up her position at the front of the milking shed, ready to be milked.

The shed was constructed so that the cows walked straight from the holding yard on to concrete ramps which ran along each side of a lowered, central aisle. Ben stepped down into this area, and moved quickly along with the hose, washing dirt and grime from the first eight cows. They would not be fed while they were in the shed. As soon as they had been milked they would be washed again, then released out to the grass in the east paddock; but, now that the late summer grass had thinned, they were also fed with hay once each day.

'I'll worry about that tomorrow,' Ben said aloud.

He had enough to worry about now. The clouds had thickened and light misty rain was falling; he was getting wet, and he wished that he had thought to wear a raincoat. Above all, he was painfully hungry.

As fast as he could, Ben clamped the suction cups on to each cow, checking that the milk pulsed up through the tubes, then channelled overhead and across to the vat in the next shed. As soon as the milk flow lessened, and stopped, he removed the suction cups, washed the cows again, then pulled the long rope that opened the gates on each side of the back of the shed.

The four cows on each ramp filed out.

'Eight!' Ben counted.

After a while he could only trust his tired brain to focus upon the endless routine of washing, fixing the suction cups, washing again, then tugging at the rope to release eight more cows. The animals were restless because they were not used to the extra waiting. They bellowed and Ben's head throbbed. As he grew more and more tired, he began to fumble, taking longer to complete each job. Once, he dropped the hose, and before he could grab it again, it coiled around to drench him, so that he was even wetter than he had been from the rain earlier.

He longed to stop the milking and forget about everything. If only he could turn all the machinery off and walk away from it all, up to the house, and change into dry clothes. And then find something to eat. His dinner. His mind dwelt more and more on food. It seemed days since he had sat with his parents in the kitchen, eating lunch. Had he missed lunch today? No, he could remember the cold beef that they had had. He could taste it. No, that had been yesterday. Today, his mother had cooked spaghetti and meatballs. Would there be anything in the fridge? His mother had not had time to tell him what to choose.

He discovered, abruptly, that he had nearly finished. He had been working too mechanically to realise that there was only one more group remaining, once he had finished the eight cows that he was milking. He looked back to the holding yard, and counted the cows. Yes, eight. And Star would be the first of this last bunch, for she had already edged into the shed, and was standing close to the animal that he was milking now. Ben felt that he had been extremely lucky, for Star was waiting quietly, even though she had lost her usual place in the milking order. He pulled thankfully down on the rope that released the back doors and, still holding the rope, he turned to re-count the last group of cows coming into the shed. The last.

Warned too late by a quick movement on his right, his head spun around; but, before he could pull the rope again to shut the exit door, Star was more than halfway through, pushing her way out with the others.

'Star!' he shouted. Uselessly.

He had only taken his eyes off her for one minute. Just that one minute, and now she was out in the paddock, unmilked. The rain drummed even more heavily on the iron roof of the milking shed as he stood, enraged. And he still had to clean all the machinery and wash out the shed before he could stop and even think about having his dinner. He would forget Star, leave her until the morning; he was simply too tired to care.

Instead, when he had finished milking the remaining seven cows, he went outside and located Star in the darkness, standing alone in the paddock. He could not take her straight back through the doors because they only opened from the inside, and perhaps Star sensed his desperation, for she made no further trouble. I suppose, Ben thought, she knows that she's punished me now for letting Bossy go first. He drove her back down the hill, and then up the race again. Star plodded along as calmly as though she normally made two trips like this every night; and Ben wallowed through the rain behind her as cold, as wet, as miserable, and as hungry as he had ever been in his life.

He milked Star in the empty shed, and it was pitch black outside before he was able to open the back door for the last time that night. He watched sourly as the Jersey walked out. He was not finished even yet. He disconnected the tubing from the stainless steel vat, disinfected the pipes, then rinsed them through with cold water. Numb with hunger and cold, he hosed down the holding yard, and then the milking shed. Finally, aching and tired, he turned off all the lights and trudged up to the house.

He had longed so desperately to get back there that he had forgotten that there would be no one to greet him; instead, darkness and utter silence met him. Even though he hurried around, switching on all the lights, the house remained unfamiliar, and almost forbidding. It was freezing as well, but he was too tired to think about heating. Slowly and painfully he stripped off the wettest of his clothes, dried himself sketchily, then opened a tin of soup and heated its contents. He cut thick slices of bread, spread them with butter, and sat eating at the large kitchen table. It was the first time that he could ever remember sitting there alone, and he found that he was not nearly as hungry as he had expected to be. He switched his gaze away from his father's chair. Where were his parents now? No one had bothered to ring him, he thought bitterly, forgetting that he would not have heard the telephone while he was down in the shed. His muscles ached. All kinds of worries pressed in on him.

If his parents didn't come back tonight – and when he remembered the blood on the bandages, he didn't think that they would – how would he manage to finish the milking in the morning in time to catch the school bus? He wondered if it would do any good to ring McGlosker; he would surely be home by now. But when Ben looked across at the telephone and thought of having to explain everything that had happened and ask for help, he felt even more exhausted. He might be better in the morning if he had a good sleep.

He had planned to set the alarm clock for six o'clock, but now he decided that he would have to allow himself an extra thirty minutes, so he adjusted the clock. He held it, listening to it ticking in the silent room.

Something would go wrong tomorrow. It would be sure to. He set it back a further half-hour.

When the alarm clock jangled next to his ear, Ben woke out of a deep sleep. The room was pitch black. The clock must be wrong, it was much too early, he thought, bewildered. But when he switched on the lamp to check the time he found that it was, indeed, five o'clock, so he swung reluctantly out of bed. He was still tired, and he wished that his head felt clearer; he didn't feel as though he'd had any sleep at all. Why did school have to begin today, of all days?

He had a quick wash and pulled on some old jeans and a shirt. He would change into his school clothes later, when he had finished the milking. His father always ate an extra, early breakfast of tea and toast before he began working in the morning; but Ben was too worried about the additional time that would take, so he decided that he would milk the cows first and eat later. The rain had stopped, but when he opened the back door and stepped outside, such an icy wind blew against him that he went back to his bedroom to get a pullover. Then he found that it was much wetter underfoot than he had expected, so he needed his gumboots, and he wasted still more valuable time going back to get them too.

After remembering this time to open the gate to the holding yard first, he sprinted down to round up the cows, flicking the torchlight on to the ground ahead as he ran. As soon as he reached the first bunch of cows he realised that it was going to be difficult to herd them at such an hour. The cows were surprised and resentful because it was still so dark; he was too early. Bossy wasted almost five precious minutes of his time, facing him with her head lowered, refusing to budge and lead the cows up for him. Finally, just when he was despairing, she turned and walked slowly and majestically up the race, bristling with indignation at every step. He was so disgusted with her that he would have given Star precedence, but she was even further down the paddock just then.

He counted the cows as they passed him, knowing that he could not rely on seeing them in the darkness if they had been left in the paddock. Two were missing. He had to run down as far as the river boundary before he found them and drove them up to join the other animals. Every few minutes he checked his watch, but he could see that he was falling behind the timetable that he had set himself, so that he had already decided, even before he had assembled all the cows in the holding yard, that he would have no chance to have his breakfast.

He switched on all the lights in the shed, but he still felt ill at ease, for the lights were placed to illuminate the milking area, and the walls of the shed disappeared in the blackness beyond. When he drove the first of the cows in, Bossy and Star both immediately dived for the front position, and on this occasion Star got there first. Bossy tried to butt the Jersey, so Ben shouted at her, and when this failed he whistled his loudest, which unexpectedly quietened her. He washed the cows and slapped on the suction cups. They were half milked before he noticed a thin trail of milk seeping along the floor. Alarmed, he raced to its source. If the machinery had broken down, he would be in real trouble.

Instead, he found that in his haste to begin he had forgotten to attach the pipes to the vat, so that all the milk had been discharging on to the floor. He rejoined the tubes, glad that he had noticed it before the milking was too far advanced, and thankful that his father would not know about the waste.

Time was racing, yet the milking machines seemed to be working painfully slowly—in a much more leisurely way than they had on the previous day. Ben had never noticed the deliberate rhythm of the motor before. Everything was going at a sluggish pace. The cows lagged back in the holding yard, so that he had to rush out of the milking shed each time to move the next batch in. Last night they had been eager enough to be milked, so that most had come into the shed without urging. Time after time he was tempted to leave the worst of the stragglers, but he kept milking, grimly noting that it was growing lighter all the time. Too quickly.

He considered leaving some of the work until later. Surely he could leave the cleaning of the sheds until he came home from school? Then he remembered that the milk tanker would be coming to collect the milk that day, and his pride would not allow him to leave the sheds dirty for the tanker driver to see and perhaps report later to his father.

He finished the cows at last. Then, in the same order that he had done the work the night before, he turned off the machines, disconnected the vat, and then hosed and cleaned, working at a feverish pace. He even ran around the sheds one final time, just to make sure that he had forgotten nothing. He turned the lights off. All the machinery was disconnected and stowed tidily away; in fact, as far as he could see, the sheds were just as clean as his father always left them.

He looked at his watch, almost afraid to check it, and his heart leapt. He had exactly twelve minutes before he must be on the road, riding his bike down to the bus stop. He could do it.

He rushed through a very perfunctory wash and changed his clothes. He broke a shoelace in his haste but managed to draw the short pieces together. It would have to do. He grabbed his bag, and the thickest piece of bread that he could find, wheeled out his bike, then pedalled furiously up to the front gate. By the time that he turned on to the road he was only four minutes later than he had planned. Not bad, he thought, I can easily make that up. He tore along the straight stretch of road, feeling almost happy. He would get to school that day, after all. Against all the odds he had succeeded. In his imagination he was already sitting in the school bus, telling the kids about his morning.

Around the corner he caught up with Mr McGlosker moving his sheep, and his heart plummeted, for the sheep were stretched in a tight mass across the road, leaving no space at all for him to pass. Ben pulled up to a crawl, wobbled along for a few metres, then had to stop and dismount. McGlosker was driving behind the mob of sheep in his utility truck, at a snail's pace, letting his two sheepdogs work the sheep along. Ben managed, after a few frantic moments, to catch his eye.

'Can I get through, please, Mr McGlosker?' he shouted urgently.

McGlosker nodded. He whistled to his dogs, and they dashed to one side of the flock, forcing the sheep over, but Ben had to walk through the gap that they made for him, raging inwardly at the extra time that it was taking. Still, he did not have far to go now. As soon as he turned the next bend in the road he would be in sight of his bus stop.

He raced around the corner, glimpsing the bus stop a few hundred metres ahead. But he also saw the back of the bus as it climbed the hill in the distance. It had been on time, and he had missed it.

Curiosity aroused

Ben rode back to the farm, bitter and despairing. He had stayed for a brief time at the bus stop, meaning to pretend to McGlosker, when the sheep reached that spot, that he was still waiting for the bus. But after a while, when McGlosker failed to appear, Ben rode slowly back and saw the sheep disappearing up a side road into the distance. He was glad about that, at least, for he had not wanted the man to be a witness to his failure.

'He'd have probably thought that I got up too late this morning,' Ben muttered miserably. It was so unfair when he'd set the alarm so much earlier, and had tried so hard.

He finished a huge and leisurely breakfast and washed the dishes, all the while thinking about the school bus that he had missed. Would his friends be wondering about him and why he hadn't caught the bus? What would it be like at school? He remembered how complacent he had been yesterday, when he had been sitting up there on top of Mount Everest. He had been so sure that he had prepared for everything, that the alarm would wake him in good time, that his mother would have his breakfast ready, that his father would have done the milking.

He could see Mount Everest from the kitchen

window, and he stood looking out at it, thinking bitterly about how it all should have been.

Yesterday. It was all so clear in his mind that he could even remember those white clouds down by the river, and the grey clouds low on the horizon. Well, he'd been right about them, anyway. It had rained all night. He recalled the electric saw, and the sudden way it had stopped. His shoulders twitched unconsciously as he thought about why it had stopped. And those crimson rosellas, and the sound of the truck coming towards him, over the hill.

The sound of the truck . . . Ben stood motionless, the towel in his hand, watching Mount Everest absently, hearing the noise of the brakes, and the skid. He saw the tarpaulin sides flapping, and the truck swinging around. The crate. He had completely forgotten it until now.

Ben put down the tea-towel that he had been holding. Surely the driver would have come back to collect his box. It would be wasting time to go and look now, to see if it was still there where it had fallen. Wasting time. Ben looked up at the kitchen clock. By now, school would have begun, and all the other kids would know exactly where their rooms were and who their teachers were. All of them would know, except him. The thought of the way he had missed the bus by just those couple of minutes made his stomach squirm, so he concentrated on the box again.

Suppose, though, that the driver had not bothered to come back? The crate might not have contained anything important or valuable enough to merit a return journey. Ben looked across at the kitchen table, testing his memory. How large had the crate been? Perhaps as wide as the kitchen table, but certainly not as long. What could it have contained? Papers? Books? If the contents were expensive, the driver would have come back, and the crate would be gone.

It had been heavy, but not so heavy that it had remained where it fell on the ground. No, it had skidded along into the bushes at the roadside. He was sure, now that he thought about the way that it had hit the road and yet remained intact, that it had not been a cardboard box. And not metal either; it had not sounded like metal. Wood. So, what would be packed in a wooden box? Tools perhaps? He felt a shiver of excitement. Guns? Could the truck driver have been a gun-runner? His brief excitement died away as he realised that the box had not looked heavy and strong enough to contain guns. Anyway, who would want guns around here? This wasn't a cowboy movie.

But he might as well go along the road and check to see if the crate was still there, because he had plenty of time now. Too much. He wondered how he was going to drag through the rest of the day until it was time to do the milking again. Before he reached the door, the telephone rang. He was so glad to hear its sharp ringing in the quiet house that he ran to answer it. Could it be the Carters?

'Hullo!' he said eagerly.

'Ben!' It was his mother's voice. 'Oh, Ben, so you didn't go to school then?' She hurried on, not waiting for a reply. 'I completely forgot that today was to be your first day at high school; we only remembered it a little while ago when Dad and I were talking. Oh Ben, I'm so sorry. What happened? Why didn't you go?'

'I missed the bus. It didn't matter,' he lied. 'It was only the first day, anyway. I'll go tomorrow.'

His mother was on a bad line, so he had to strain to hear her. He thought that she asked if he was all right.

'Yes, Mum. I'm fine. How's Dad?'

'Just a minute.' The phone jangled, then her voice became a little clearer. 'I've put some more money in, but I'm afraid that I've got no more change after this lot, I forgot to get any more, I was so anxious to find out whether you'd managed to get to school. I suppose that I was hoping that no one would answer, and then I'd know that you got away all right.' Ben's question seemed to register at last. 'He's going to have an operation this afternoon. Not a serious one; they're going to do a little microsurgery on his hand so that his fingers won't be affected by the accident. Oh, and Ben, they weren't able to operate at Coonara, so they've sent us on to Sydney.'

Sydney! Ben swallowed hard. He had thought that they were only a few kilometres away, at the Coonara Hospital. Sydney. It was a long way. The telephone line sputtered again, and he missed a couple of words.

'−be perfectly all right, but he might have to stay here a few more days, I'm afraid. Oh, there's the red light coming up again on this phone, so I'll have to go. Are you sure that you'll be all right, Ben? I tried to ring the Carters, before.'

'I'm fine, Mum,' he said. 'Don't worry.'

He did not know if she heard, for the dial tone rasped in his ear so he knew that they had been disconnected. He weighed the phone in his hand for a moment, not wanting to lose his contact with her, then he replaced it, feeling rather forlorn. She had mentioned the Carters, and he wondered if he should try them again. Perhaps later, after he had looked for that box.

He had to postpone the search for a short time because the huge milk tanker had arrived and was snaking down the driveway. It clattered across the cattlegrid, described a wide circle, then came to a halt beside the milking shed. Ben knew the man by sight. He was in a hurry.

'I've got to do an extra run this morning,' he called to Ben. 'One of our tankers broke down yesterday, and

24

they're waiting for some parts to be sent from Sydney to fix it.'

He wasted no time connecting the tanker's hoses to the vat, then proceeded to transfer the milk over to the tanker. As soon as he had finished, he gave Ben a receipt, waved, and drove off. So I needn't have done all that cleaning this morning after the milking, Ben thought, staring resentfully after him. The driver was too busy to notice anything. I could have saved all that time, and then I'd have caught the bus easily. And I'd have caught the bus anyway, if McGlosker and his stupid sheep hadn't been on the road, the way they were.

Ben trudged slowly up to the gate. He climbed over it to save having to open and refasten it, then he headed along the road towards the Mount Everest corner, walking at the edge of the road. The wind that had chilled him that morning had blown the rain away, and it had become much warmer. Now the air was very still and he could hear someone chopping rhythmically, away in the distance; it was probably McGlosker. The remoteness of the sound made him feel even more isolated, and he wondered, uneasily, if anyone at all would hear him if he needed to call for help.

A kookaburra set up an abrupt clamour in the trees ahead, but it petered out after a few seconds, as though discouraged. It grew very quiet again, except for the crunching sound of his shoes on the road and the distant chopping. Suddenly, he wished quite desperately that he had managed to catch the school bus that morning.

I shouldn't have bothered about the milking at all, he told himself. I should have gone to school instead. Why had his father had an accident now, to spoil everything? Then, for the first time, a chilling idea struck him: would his father really get better? Had his mother told him the truth? He bent down to pick up a stone, and as he sent it skipping along the road ahead he was reminded of the way that the box had skidded from the truck yesterday. He walked a little faster because he could see the hairpin bend clearly now.

When he reached the corner he looked for the box first of all at the side of the road approximately where he thought that he had seen it vanish. He had passed this spot in the car with his parents many times, but had never noticed how densely the trees grew. He found, too, that a view from the level of the roadway was quite different from the picture that he had gained when gazing down from Mount Everest.

Uncertain now, he looked back over his shoulder towards the hill, trying to estimate his position again. The crate had come off here, he was sure of that. He traced it in his imagination, seeing it topple, fall, then slide across the road. It should certainly be around here somewhere, unless the driver had come back to retrieve it. Was there any sign on the road; a skid mark, or broken bushes beside the road? He scanned the road's surface very carefully, but if the crate had made any scratches or lines, last night's rain had obliterated them. Even the truck's skid marks were almost gone.

The bushes at the side of the road gave him no clue either. When he walked over to them and parted them hesitantly, he could see nothing but dark greenery through the tangled branches. Ben scuffed his toes abstractedly on the road, wondering what he should do and whether it was worth bothering about. It was disappointing because he had expected that the box would be easy to find; but then, nothing that he expected seemed to be happening lately, only the unexpected. After a short wait he decided that, since he had walked this far along the road and he had nothing else to do anyway, he would investigate a little further. There was nothing to stop him, for the land was unfenced. No one could accuse him of trespassing if he explored it.

He pushed cautiously in amongst the bracken and the trees. Damp leaves brushed his face. He watched the ground ahead of him very carefully as he moved along. A thought shivered in his mind. McGlosker had killed a couple of tiger snakes recently on his land; he had draped them across his front gate in the time-honoured way, displaying them to warn his neighbours that they, too, should watch for them.

The ground dipped very sharply, and it was slippery from last night's rain. Ben halted, suddenly reluctant to proceed. It would be useless to look further, he argued silently, because it was obvious that there was nothing here; the driver must have come back to collect his box after all. He took a couple more steps, then stopped again. Had he heard something? He waited for another moment, uneasy, straining to hear. The silence was menacing. Even the wood-chopping had ceased. The sun, barely filtering through the trees, shrouded the trees with a sinister curtain of leaves. He started off once more, finding that he was breathing a little faster.

There it was again! Ben stood anchored to the ground, trying to recall the noise, to recognise it. Such a brief sound, had it come from in front of him, there? Or from behind him? He waited, his heart pounding. Nothing. Just this damp stillness. He ventured to move again. One slow step forward, then a quicker one. Another.

Something stirred and scuffled, and Ben froze. Something was there, close to him. He couldn't see it, but it was there. He panicked. Turning to run, his foot caught against something large and solid, and he tripped and sprawled heavily in the mud. He was on his feet again in an instant, but as he began to run back towards the road, he saw more clearly what he had stumbled over. The crate. The noise that had frightened him had come from inside the crate.

An
unexpected find

Ben did not wait to investigate. He scrambled back up to the road as fast as he could, glad to reach the warm sunshine and leave the shadowy bush behind him. He stood there, feeling a little foolish in the brightness, and brushed the mud from his jeans very energetically, to cover his confusion. What should he do now? Already his commonsense was arguing that it was only a box, and no matter what was confined there, it could not get out. It was still in the box, so no matter how dangerous it was, it had not been able to escape.

Should he go back and look again? Surely there was no danger if he merely looked? He would not have to touch the box at all, and he certainly had no intention of opening it. He looked back along the road to the farm, half wishing that someone would come driving along that way, so that he could stop them and ask them to come with him to look at what he had found. Perhaps he should just leave the box where it was and go back to the farm, and forget all about it.

Undecided, he considered this while he waited, sitting at the side of the road with his back against a gum tree, half-heartedly pitching stones at the bushes opposite. But no one came. At last he grew tired of waiting. He stood up, turned, and plunged down towards the crate again, trying to forget about the tiger snakes and bending low to avoid the prickling branches that clutched and scratched him.

Now that he knew exactly where to look, it was easy to trace the path that the box had taken down the slope; and, when he reached it, to see how it had overturned at the last into a mass of bracken. And now that he was closer to it, it looked so bulky that he wondered how he could have missed seeing it earlier. Still from a cautious distance, he studied the wooden box, wishing that its size could give him some clue to its contents. It was about a metre high, but it was hard to be certain about its length because one end of it was covered by the bracken.

He racked his brains to think what a box of that size might contain. It was too small for an animal like a sheep, for example. What, then? He strained to hear if anything still moved inside it, and he tried to remember the sound that he had heard before; but it had been too fleeting, hardly a sound at all.

Circling the box carefully he found the outline of an emu stencilled on the side; but he knew that the crate could not possibly contain an emu because it was not large enough. When he looked closer, he saw that the stencil was actually part of an address – Emu River, South Australia, and a telephone number. South Australia was a long way from where the box had fallen, but he could ring them and tell them the box was here, couldn't he?

Although it was so dark there amongst the trees, Ben believed that it might be possible to get a better view – safely – if he could only stand the crate upright. He scouted around until he found a thick, straight branch, then he clambered in amongst the bracken to wedge it behind the box so that he could lever it up. That done, he jammed the branch firmly at the back of the crate to hold it steady and as level as possible on the slope.

He paused, listening. All the time that he had been

working he had heard nothing. Perhaps that earlier sound had been something that he had merely imagined. At any rate, since he had been able to move the box so easily, whatever was inside was neither large nor heavy. And definitely not alive either, because there had been complete silence while he shifted it.

He had no sooner assured himself of this when he noticed something else. Part of the wooden side that had lain in the bracken had been cut away and replaced by wire netting. He had become so curious that he grew bolder, encouraged by the continued silence from within the crate, and he moved closer, trying to peer through the netting. If I hear anything slithering inside there, he promised himself, I'll leave everything just as it is and go back and ring McGlosker. It was hard to tell, in the dimness, if there was anything there at all. Had he really heard that noise before? He had to know. He pressed his face against the wire netting.

Concentrating, he made out a small, dark creature, huddled in a ball at the back of the crate. Could it be a possum? A cat? Then he heard the rustling noise again, and something more. A whimper. It was a dog.

A dog! Ben slanted his head to allow a little more light to fall into the box. He could see it now, a small animal, not much more than a puppy really, and very frightened. Ben gave a very soft whistle, trying not to alarm it even more.

'You poor little thing,' he said. 'You've been here all night. Without any food.'

The ground beneath the box was wet and muddy, so the dog may have been able to find a little water during the night, but Ben winced as he recalled the way that the box had thudded on to the road.

'I hope you're not hurt.'

He had to work fast and get the dog out as quickly as he could. Checking the sides of the box to see if he could wrench them open, he saw that they were quite sturdy and still firmly nailed, so he would need a hammer. He raced back along the road, scaled the front gate and ran down along the drive past the farmhouse to the toolshed, where he selected a handful of tools; the hammer from above the workbench, a screwdriver and a small saw. If I can't prise those sides off, he thought, I'll have to saw them off. I can't leave the dog there.

When he returned he peered anxiously through the wire netting, but the dog looked as though it had not moved since he had left it. In fact, it was so still that—for one heart-stopping moment—Ben thought that it might have died while he had been gone. But when he examined it more closely, he was relieved to see the dog's side rising and falling very faintly as it breathed.

'This won't take long,' Ben promised.

Using the claw of the hammer he lifted a couple of the boards from the front, near the bottom of the box, then wrenched them off as quietly as he could, fearful that the noise that he was making was adding to the dog's fear.

'There you are. Out you come!' Ben called, as soon as he had made enough room for the dog to wriggle out. He wished that he knew its name.

It did not respond, but remained huddled in the corner. Ben wondered if he should simply reach in and pull the dog out; but he was reluctant because he thought that the animal might turn and bite him, since it was obviously so upset. Eventually, however, after endless coaxing, he found that it was the only thing that he could do, so he stretched an arm through the gap that he had made, gripped the dog as gently and firmly as possible, and hauled it out. It offered no resistance; it was trembling, and he cradled it against his chest protectively.

'I'm going to take you home with me,' he whispered. 'Don't worry, you're going to be all right.'

Ben walked back along the road towards the farmhouse with the small bundle in his arms. He felt glad, for the first time that day, that there was so little traffic along the road. Adults had a habit of interfering, and he did not want anyone to take the dog away from him. As he walked, he spoke very softly, to try to calm it.

'Don't worry. I'll keep you just for a little while, until you feel better.'

His mind was already racing with plans. He would have to find some food to give the dog, of course. It was not a large dog, although it was getting heavier as he walked along and it kept slipping from his grasp because he was carrying it awkwardly. He paused to adjust his hold, trying to make the dog comfortable, but painfully aware that it was still trembling. He felt that it should have known that it was safe with him.

He wondered how he was going to open the front gate, because merely holding the dog steady took so much effort, but he managed to lift the wire tie by taking the animal's weight more on to one arm than the other, and fumbling blindly with the hand that this manoeuvre had freed.

As he moved the latch he caught sight of his hand. It was covered in blood. The dog was hurt, perhaps badly.

Ben kicked the gate shut behind him, and began to run awkwardly along the driveway, cradling the dog against his chest, trying desperately to keep it steady. The vet, he thought. He must ring the vet. When he reached the house he placed the dog very gently down on the verandah in the sun, with a vague feeling that the animal should be kept warm. He hurried inside and rinsed the blood from his hand, then he ran to the telephone. It seemed to take ages before he managed to find the vet's number, and when he began to dial his fingers were shaking so much that he had to stop halfway and start again. He expected the voice of the woman who always sat in the office, but it was Dr Wallace himself who answered.

'Ben? Yes, Ben. One of the cows, is it?'

'No. It's a dog.' Ben explained quickly that he had found it on the road. 'It's injured. It's bleeding.'

'I'll come right away,' the vet said. 'Don't worry, Ben, I'll be there in about ten minutes.'

Ben hurried back to the verandah. The dog had not stirred, as far as he could tell, so he sat down beside it, stroking it gently while he kept watch on the small strip of road that he could glimpse past the front gate. He willed Dr Wallace to come quickly. Once, he half rose to his feet when he saw a small white car approaching, but he subsided again when the car sped by. A few minutes later he caught sight of another car, a large blue one; and to his relief, this one slowed, then stopped at the gate while Dr Wallace got out of the car to open it. Another minute, and the vet was standing beside him on the verandah, gazing down at the dog.

'You found him on the road, did you?' he asked Ben. 'I don't think that he's a local dog.'

Dr Wallace squatted down on the verandah, his hands moving slowly over the animal, pressing and testing. The dog hardly moved. Ben watched Dr Wallace's face as he worked, wishing that the man would tell him quickly what was wrong.

'Is he going to be OK?' he asked, when he found that he could bear the waiting no longer.

Dr Wallace turned the dog gently over on its side, and Ben caught his breath when he saw the blood on the dog's coat. The vet heard him and looked up. He smiled sympathetically.

'I can't find any broken bones,' he said, probing the

dog's side gently. 'He's been badly knocked about though, and he's got a nasty lump on this side. That's probably his worst problem. And there's a cut, just there.' He pointed, although Ben did not need to be shown. 'I'll give him an injection in case of infection, but it should heal quite well without any stitching.'

He sat back on his heels and looked the dog over critically. 'I said that lump was the worst problem, but I don't know—the shock he's had, that was bad. He's going to need a lot of rest, and reassurance.' He was busy with a syringe for a moment, then, very casually, 'Where did you say you found him?'

Ben hesitated. He was sorely tempted to say that the dog was a stray, and that he had found it wandering on the road. If he mentioned the crate he might be told to ring the owner immediately; or worse, the vet might ring the owner himself. But he realised that he must give an honest account of the way that the dog had been hurt, so that Dr Wallace would know how to treat him. Ben explained precisely what he had seen from Mount Everest, and exactly how the crate had thudded on to the road.

'D' you mean to tell me that the crate was in a truck with a tarpaulin over it?' the vet asked, and when Ben nodded, Dr Wallace said, 'I can't understand that at all. I've seen the way they transport their dogs from Emu Creek. Those crates, for example, they were specially designed by a vet. They take a lot of care with those dogs.' He noted Ben's frown, and continued. 'A dog is better travelling in something secure, otherwise it might escape and get lost, or run over; there's all sorts of possibilities.'

'It could be on a lead, or something,' Ben muttered.

'Even a lead can be dangerous, especially since most people don't know how to handle a dog on a lead. No, what I can't understand is why they allowed the dog to be transported in a truck like that, under a tarpaulin. What about the heat? How could you be sure that the dog would have enough air?' Dr Wallace rose to his feet. 'Why didn't the driver come back last night? If he lost the box soon after lunch, he would have noticed that it'd gone when he went to give the dog water.' A very long pause. 'Unless, of course, he hadn't bothered about that.'

Dr Wallace stood looking up towards the road, his lips drawn tight. Then he turned to Ben. 'Look, Ben, I can promise you that the dog's going to be all right. Just keep him quiet and warm, and try to build up his confidence. I'm sorry, but I've got to hurry away now. When you rang me I was just leaving for my holidays; you were the very last call.' He shut his bag. 'If you do have any problems with him, you can ring the young fellow who'll be filling in for me. I'm sure that you won't have to, though.'

Stammering his thanks, Ben tried to remember how much Dr Wallace usually charged for a visit; he was not sure if he would be able to find enough money in the house. But the vet was already on his way.

'No charge,' he called back over his shoulder.

He did not drive away at once. He came back from his car carrying a large plastic bag.

'Here you are, Ben,' he said. 'I've been carting this around for days in the car.' He placed the bag on the verandah. 'It's a packet of dog food pellets; the manufacturers are always sending me samples. You may as well have it. Give the dog the amount that's shown on the packet. Oh, and plenty of water, of course; always make sure that he has as much water as he wants.'

He was gone before Ben could thank him again. The boy could hardly believe his good luck. Dr Wallace was leaving for his holidays, so he had been too busy to ask after Ben's parents, and the immediate problem of the dog's food had been miraculously solved.

Keep him quiet and warm, Dr Wallace had said. In that case, Ben argued, it might be best to move the dog indoors, for although it was warm enough now while the sun was out, the nights were usually chilly. At first he considered getting a box from the shed to make a bed, but then he decided against that, because he thought that the dog might have had more than enough experience of boxes. Instead, he made up a rough bed in a corner of the kitchen using an old rug, then he carried the dog carefully inside and settled him down very gently. When he had finished, the animal looked quite comfortable, and although he was still lying in a tight, tense ball, he had at last stopped trembling.

'I wish I knew your name,' Ben said.

Was there a popular name for sheepdogs? He tried to remember what McGlosker called his dogs, but their names eluded him. He tried a few aloud, but the dog did not stir. Ben felt that he was listening intently, even though he did not respond.

Ben tried to get a clue to his name from his appearance. He was similar to McGlosker's two sheepdogs, but slightly smaller because he was obviously younger. He was a darker colour though, almost all black, with just a little tan colouring around his eyes.

'Darkie?' Ben tried. 'Blackie?'

The dog ignored him. What else could he try? The dog, like McGlosker's two, was a kelpie, the Australian sheepdog, but Ben could not think of any dog's name that would stem from that fact.

'I wish you could talk,' Ben told the dog, giving up at last.

Since it was well past lunchtime he made some sandwiches, and sat at the table munching them and watching the dog. Was the dog hungry too? As soon as he had finished he would put some of the pellets that the vet had given him close to the dog. He might be able to tempt him to eat. And some water, of course, because the vet had been very insistent about the water.

'I'll have you fighting fit in no time,' Ben promised the dog.

He reflected on the strange morning that he had spent; everything had turned out quite differently from what he had expected. He remembered that after he had spoken to his mother, he had wondered how he would fill in the day, but he had been so busy that he had almost forgotten about missing the school bus. He rinsed his plate and cup, dried them and stacked them away, then he went to the door to get the bucket from the verandah. As he opened the door a flash of light up on the road caught his eye. It was the tourist coach, late as always, speeding in the direction of Coonara. And close behind it—much too close for safety—raced the truck, its green tarpaulin still loosely flapping in the wind.

Covering
the tracks

The coach and the truck were both well out of sight along the road before Ben was able to draw breath. When he found that he could move again he shut and locked the door, even while he knew that it was a futile gesture. After all, what could he do to stop the truck driver taking the dog away, if he came to the farm and asked for it? Ben's hand clenched on the key. If he admitted that the dog was there in the kitchen, the driver would take him away in the truck. Ben remembered how the dog had shuddered as he carried him back along the road, and what an age it had been before he had stopped trembling.

Ben knew that he could not tell the driver that the dog was here; not a driver who drove like that; not a driver who rarely checked to see if the dog needed water. Ben remembered the vet's wrathful expression. No, Ben thought. I won't tell the driver that the dog is here. I can't tell him.

Ben unlocked the door and opened it just a little to peer cautiously up towards the road. The driver had obviously found the dog missing; that was why he had come back along the road, to see if he could find him. He had gone past this time, but how much further would he travel before he turned? How long before he came back?

When he returned, he would be certain to stop at the Mount Everest corner to look for the crate. There would be few corners as sharp as that one, few other places along the road where he could have lost it. Ben groaned aloud as he remembered how he had whistled to attract the driver's attention yesterday; the man would be sure to remember it too. He would stop his truck at the corner and search. He would find the crate as Ben had, but broken.

Ben stood, his eyes straining towards the empty stretch of road. Empty for how long? His mind was jammed at a dead stop, fixed on a vision of the box as he had left it, with its side wrenched open. No one could imagine that a dog could have escaped in such a manner, so the driver would come and enquire at the nearest farm. He would know that someone must have opened the crate and taken the dog away. He would know, just as soon as he saw it.

Ben's mind was beginning to flutter, and stir again. Yes, the driver would know as soon as he saw it. But what if he never saw it? What if the crate was gone when he went to look for it? Wouldn't he believe, then, that he must have lost it somewhere else? Surely it would be possible to take the crate to pieces, and then load them on to the wheelbarrow and bring them back to the farm.

Ben had already begun to run towards the shed, but he stopped. No, he thought, frustrated, a wheelbarrow would be too cumbersome, too slow, and he might be seen wheeling it back along the road when the truck returned. He would be caught then, red-handed. What else could he do? What would be the quickest way to dispose of the crate? Ben forced himself to stand still and save precious energy, while he thought.

He remembered that the crate had been much further from the road than he had expected it to be.

His mind almost raced past that thought, but now it braked, reversed, and waited while he reflected. It had been so far from the road that he had nearly given up looking for it, hadn't he? Therefore, if he could somehow shift the crate even further from the road, the driver might abandon the search. Even if he did not have enough time to bring the box back to the farm and hide it, surely he could push it further down the slope and completely out of sight before the driver came back?

He ran again. First, down to the shed to collect an axe, then, instead of heading up the drive and along the road, he raced straight across the front pastures and past the dam, heading towards Mount Everest but keeping clear of the road. When he reached the end of their property he scaled the fence, then, after making certain that the truck was not approaching, he dashed across the road and plunged down through the trees.

The crate was still lying there, but he could see at once that he would not be able to roll it down the slope as he had hoped; it was much too bulky and it would catch against the trees. He stood looking at it, his heart sinking. What else could he do? What would be the quickest way to dispose of it? He remembered the axe. He would break the crate into three or four pieces, small enough to throw into the bracken. Did he have time?.

Holding the axe tightly, his hands damp with fear, he listened intently, struggling to hear the sound of the truck's engine. How long did he have? Seconds? Minutes? A parrot crackled hoarsely from amongst the trees, then stopped. In the hush he waited just one more moment, then he raised the axe.

Crash! He stopped, petrified. The noise! They must be able to hear it for miles. But what else could he do? And wouldn't it sound like someone chopping firewood, anyway? He summoned up all his courage and swung the axe again, faster this time, smashing it down again and again.

In a few minutes it was done. He threw down the axe and gathered up the splintered pieces of the crate. He set aside those that had any lettering on them; he would take them home to decipher later. The rest he hurled down the slope into the thickest bracken that he could see. Then he stood, as the driver might stand soon, looking down in that direction. Nothing showed.

Next, he worked feverishly to cover up the marks that the crate had made when it skidded down the slope. It was easier than he had expected. He tore a couple of branches from the nearest gum tree and then drew them backwards and forwards across the soft earth to erase all the traces. He left the branches lying there; the trees were so dense that the extra branches did not look amiss on the ground. All the time, he was listening.

After one final, desperate, searching gaze around to see if he had forgotten anything, he collected the small pieces of wood that he had set aside, and the axe; then he struggled quickly back up to the road and straight across it. He climbed the fence and began to hurry back to the farmhouse, taking the same route that he had chosen earlier, anxious to get out of sight as quickly as possible.

He had barely passed the dam when he heard the sound of the truck's engine. He looked down, appalled, at the pieces of the crate that he was carrying; his guilt made them assume the size of towers. He dropped them, and the axe, on the ground and, turning quickly towards the dam, he sent a couple of stones sailing in a wide, high arc to plop down into the middle of the dam. It was, he hoped, a perfect image of someone with nothing on his mind and nothing much to do, but he was shaking so much that he had to sit down on the grass as soon as the stones had left his hand. He watched the family of ducks that lived near the dam scuttering indignantly across the water. He dared not look towards the road. He heard the truck stop at the corner.

Ben held his breath, waiting. The door of the truck banged loudly. The driver must have got out; he would be checking to see if the crate was there. Unable to remain still a moment longer, Ben sprang to his feet, gathered up the pieces of wood and the axe, and strolled in the direction of the house as nonchalantly as his shaky legs would allow him. He longed to turn his head and look back towards the corner to see what was happening, but he did not dare. He wanted to rush back to the house and lock himself safely inside with the dog, but he was too afraid that he might draw the truck driver's attention if he hurried. So he walked; but he was so frightened that, by the time he reached the kitchen again, he was breathing as heavily as if he had dashed all the way at top speed.

He waited for a long while just inside the locked front door, with his ear pressed against the wood, listening intently. It seemed to be quiet for an eternity, then he heard the truck's engine roar away into the distance.

Ben relaxed at last. If the driver had found any trace, he would have come to the farm to make enquiries. Now everything would be all right, for the man had checked the corner and he had found nothing. He would not come back this way again.

The dog was asleep, still huddled in a tight ball in the corner where Ben had placed him, in the quiet and warmth of the kitchen. Ben remembered that he had not brought in the food and water as he had intended, because he had been interrupted by the arrival of the truck, so he hurried now to arrange the pellets on a dish and the water in a bucket. He placed them as close as possible to the dog, then waited for a few minutes, but the dog did not appear to have noticed any of this activity and was apparently still asleep.

While he waited he set out on the table those pieces

of the crate that he had salvaged, and examined them curiously. Neatly stamped on one was the Emu River address and a telephone number. I suppose that I really should ring them now, Ben thought, fingering the wood, but he made no move towards the telephone, and finally he pushed the piece of wood aside. I'll do it later, he decided, perhaps tomorrow; the dog might be a little better tomorrow.

A second piece of wood showed an address further along the coast, on the other side of Sydney. After reading it dubiously several times Ben placed it beside the first.

He picked up the third piece. The printing on it had been too indistinct to read when he had been back there amongst the trees, and even now it was hard to decipher. Someone had scratched some words on the wood in pencil, and after a great deal of difficulty he made out the first two. 'Eight months.' That would be the dog's age, he guessed. The third word was even more difficult to make sense of. He twisted the wood around and around in his hand, holding it up to catch the light and spelling out each letter aloud as he made certain of it.

'Charcoal.' Charcoal? Could that be the dog's name? He looked at the lettering doubtfully, checking it again. Charcoal. It seemed an odd name for a dog, though. He looked across at the dog, then walked over and knelt beside it.

'Charcoal,' he said, trying it out, but uncertainly.

The dog gave no sign that it had heard, so Ben stood up to return to the table, but as he moved he saw the dog's ears twitch upright, although its eyes were still shut.

'Charcoal,' Ben said again, more confidently.

This time, there was no mistaking the dog's reaction. The ears twitched again. One eye opened, and then shut. Delighted, Ben sat down on the floor beside him and stroked his coat gently. He felt the dog give a long sigh, and then a little shiver, and his heart contracted. Poor little thing, Ben thought, he's still terrified after his experience in the crate.

He realised with a shock that he had given no thought to school for hours – not since breakfast. And, even more surprising, he felt quite glad that McGlosker's sheep had been on the road that morning so that he had missed the school bus. Otherwise, he would not have remembered the crate and the truck driver would have recovered it instead and taken the dog away before he was fit to travel. I'll ring the dog's owner tomorrow, Ben promised himself. There'll be plenty of time tomorrow.

The dog suddenly uncurled, rested his head on Ben's ankle, then went to sleep again. Ben sat quietly, not daring to move; he must not disturb the dog, which looked relaxed at last. He sat while the sun faltered behind the kitchen curtains and then disappeared. The milking was due to be done again. The dog seemed to be sleeping quite soundly now, so Ben moved his leg very gently, climbed carefully to his feet, and tiptoed out. He had made a decision while he had waited beside the dog. He would not go to school tomorrow; instead, he would stay at home and look after Charcoal for one more day.

When he went down to gather the herd together he found that the cows were still irritable and unhappy. They were used to a set pattern of handling; they were very content with routine. Although Bossy and Star were still fighting each other for the lead, the rest of the herd had long before sorted out their own order of precedence. In his haste and anxiety, Ben had disturbed that order, and unsettled them. This time he allowed them to proceed more slowly and in their own way, so

44

that he managed to complete the milking without accident. As he returned to the house, he heard the phone ringing.

'Ben!' His mother's voice sounded very close this time. 'I've been ringing off and on for the last hour, but I suppose that you've been out with the Carters, milking. I hoped I'd catch you before it got too late. Ben, the operation went very well.'

'Great!'

'We'll probably only have to stay here one more day, I think. Two, at the most. How are you getting on? Are you having plenty to eat?'

'Sure.'

'I rang the school, dear, and told them about the accident, and the headmaster was very nice. He said that you're not to worry, and he'll make sure that you don't miss anything. And Ben—can you hear, Ben?'

'Yes, Mum.'

'I've remembered that there're some frozen dinners on the left-hand side of the freezer; they're wrapped in foil, you can't miss them. They were for emergencies. You only have to put them in the oven to heat. Are you sure that you're managing all right?'

'Oh yes, Mum. I am, really.'

He was distracted. He could hear a scrabbling noise behind him, and when he turned around he found Charcoal standing in the doorway, looking at him with bright eyes.

'I hope that you've thanked Mr Carter for his help, Ben.' Then, as Ben stood, uncertain how to answer, 'I can't hear you very well, Ben.'

'Sorry, Mum.'

Charcoal was standing close, looking up at him, and Ben bent down to rub his head. He decided not to worry his mother about the Carters.

'We hope to be home really soon, Ben,' his mother

said. 'Now, make sure that you have enough to eat, won't you?'

'Yes. Oh, and tell Dad not to worry about a thing. Everything's going just fine here. And the tanker came for the milk this morning.' That seemed to have happened so long ago that he nearly forgot to mention it.

'I'll tell him. 'Bye, dear.'

While his dinner was heating Ben took Charcoal outside, but the animal was still too nervous to stray far, preferring to move around in little, uncertain circles, investigating. Ben left him alone, hoping that he would gain confidence, and sat waiting for him on the verandah step. It was dark but clear of clouds now, so that the stars plastered the sky thickly, very close above Ben's head. When he visited his grandfather he often watched the stars in the city, but there they seemed remote and not as familiar and as friendly as they did above the farm. In the quietness he could hear the pallid cuckoo's mournful whistle rising note after note up the scale.

After a while, mindful of the vet's instructions, Ben rose and took Charcoal back inside the house once more. 'You've got to be kept warm, the vet says,' he told the dog. 'And anyway, I've got to eat, you know.'

And eat he did. For some reason he was much hungrier than he had been the night before; and, although the frozen dinner that he had chosen was marked 'for two' he had no trouble finishing it off. Then, still hungry, he made some sandwiches and drank two glasses of milk. All the time that he was eating, Charcoal lay watching him intently.

'I'm going to stay home with you tomorrow,' Ben said, and he was sure that the dog understood, because he saw him wag his tail for the first time. Then, feeling a little guilty about school, he added, 'There're some jobs that I still have to do, like that extra feeding for the cows.'

When Ben woke in the morning he found Charcoal asleep beside his bed. Some time during the night the dog must have left the kitchen and pushed the bedroom door open to reach Ben. He looked so secure and peaceful that Ben chose to lie in bed a little longer in order not to disturb him. He could use the time to plan the coming day. While Ben watched him, Charcoal stirred, and though still asleep, he made little yipping noises. He's chasing sheep, Ben thought, smiling.

He was reluctant to leave the warmth of his bed, so he lay thinking. Even though he had already decided before his mother rang last night that he would stay home with Charcoal one more day, he was glad that she had rung the school. First of all today, he must do the milking, and as soon as he had finished that, he would take the truck around the paddocks to distribute the supplementary feed. He felt a stir of apprehension at the thought, but he fought it down. He had never started the truck himself, or been wholly responsible for it. He had driven it, of course, but always with his father beside him. He tried to imagine the look on his father's face when he learned that Ben had managed to do the whole lot by himself. Let's hope that I can, Ben thought. When all the work was done, he could spend the rest of the day with Charcoal.

He was aroused from these pleasant thoughts by a loud banging on the back door. Charcoal's head swung around sharply, and he looked up at Ben as the boy slid out of bed and struggled into his dressing-gown. It isn't that driver back, Ben assured himself. He won't be back anymore. It's so early, barely seven-thirty. Perhaps it's Mr Carter. He shut the door to the bedroom, glad that the dog had wandered in there last night, and hurried to the back door. He found his friend Julie standing there, holding her bike.

'Ben!' She looked anxious. 'You're not ready. You

didn't come to school yesterday. Are you sick?'

She looked at her watch, and Ben realised that she must have cycled out from Coonara at this early hour to find out what had happened. Julie lived in the town, next to the bank. He should have rung her last night to tell her what had happened, but he had been too tired to think.

'No. I'm not sick. It's Dad—he's had an accident. He cut his hand on the power saw and he had to go to hospital. Mum went with him, so I'm doing all the milking, and looking after the farm.'

She looked just as impressed as he had hoped. 'Are you doing all right?'

'Uh-huh. Anyway, they'll be back soon. Probably today, I think.'

'You can't come to school today, then?'

'I don't think it'll matter if I stop home another day.'

It was funny, that. He had been worried and upset yesterday about missing school, but now it seemed far more important to care for Charcoal. He hesitated. Would he tell her about the dog? Julie had no time left, however; she was checking her watch again.

'I've got to get back home,' she said. 'I've only had half my breakfast, and I don't want to miss the bus. Look, it doesn't matter about school, we're only sorting ourselves out—you know, finding out where the classrooms are, and all that. We'll show you tomorrow; you're not missing much. I'll tell the kids what you're doing.' She waved. 'See you.'

But she had only pedalled a short distance before she turned back. 'I can't come and help, Ben,' she explained. 'Not unless you're still away on Thursday. I could come then, if you like. My cousins are coming over this afternoon because it's Dad's birthday, and tomorrow Mum's taking me over to Jindagery after school.'

48

'I'll be right,' Ben protested, pleased that she had offered, but even more pleased to think that he really did not need any help. Julie was great, and he was sorry that he hadn't had the time to tell her about Charcoal. He stood watching until she was just a speck in the distance, and then he went back inside.

A new companion

As soon as Ben had dressed he took the dog out for a quick run, then he shut him back inside the house. He was not sure how Charcoal would behave when faced with the herd, and he did not want any trouble with the cows now that everything was going so well with the milking. He was surprised how well he was managing. This morning it was done without incident again. Because he had now learned not to hurry them, the cows were more relaxed, and Bossy and Star skirmished only briefly. When he had finished, double-checking that he had forgotten nothing, he went back to the house very cheerfully to have his breakfast.

He found that Charcoal had already eaten all the food that had been put out for him, so Ben gave him some more and then replenished his water bucket. Surely now that Charcoal was eating so well, it was a sign that the dog was much better. And he was beginning to look more confident too. Today was going to be a really great day.

As soon as breakfast was finished he began to prepare for the job that he had been looking forward to; thoughts of it had been bubbling happily at the back of his mind ever since he had woken that morning. This time, Ben took Charcoal with him. At first he had left the dog in the house, but when he was halfway to the shed he changed his mind, and went back to let him out. It was such a beautiful sunny morning that it seemed unkind not to let Charcoal share it with him.

Today he was going to drive the truck. His father always parked it in the largest shed where the stacked hay was stored, and the key was usually left in the ignition. The boy, with Charcoal close beside him, walked through the small orchard at the back of the house and crunched across the broken almond shells that spattered the grass circling the almond tree. The galahs had flown in to strip the tree a few days earlier, covering the tree like a rippling grey and pink shawl as they plucked and opened the nuts. His father had wanted to frighten them off, but his mother would not allow him to disturb them.

'The birds are too beautiful,' she said. 'And they're only taking the nuts that we haven't been able to reach. There's plenty of almonds for us all.'

Charcoal was an ideal companion, quiet and always close by. When Ben reached the truck and opened its door, it seemed the most natural thing in the world for the dog to jump up and sit on the seat beside the driver's.

'You've done this before,' Ben observed.

Ben heaved the bales of hay up on to the tray of the truck. Usually this would have been a job for two people; he had often helped his father. Then, his father drove and Ben, sitting on the back of the truck, shoved a bale of hay off every fifty metres or so, as they moved across the paddocks. Since he had to work by himself today, he would have to pull up at intervals, get out of the truck, then go to the back to toss the hay off.

First, though, he must start the truck. He had watched his father often enough to know how it was done, but when he tried it now, he found that the past cold nights had made the engine sluggish, so that his rather tentative efforts died miserably away. He sat fingering the car keys, staring out the windscreen, already faintly discouraged. Should he abandon the entire project? But if he did, it would mean that the cows would not get the extra feed, and the milk production would be down. He sat forward and turned the key again. Again, the engine would not catch. All right, he thought, suddenly reckless, just one more try, even if it does flatten the battery. Because it was to be the last, he stamped the accelerator hard to the floor, and waited. The engine roared.

He put the truck carefully into low gear, and it jolted forward over the rough paddock. He decided that he would stay in first gear all the time; he did not have to hurry because it did not matter how long he took to finish the work. The only worry he had now was that he must take care not to stall the truck whenever he stopped to push the hay off the back.

He found the work absorbing. The cows were scattered in little groups across the paddocks, so he drove as close as he could to where they gathered and stopped the truck, first making sure that the motor would not cut out. Then he got out of the truck and tossed the bales of hay on to the grass. He enjoyed it immensely. He could only guess at the number of bales he needed for each group, but he felt that it would not hurt the cows if he calculated wrongly.

Like everything else that he had attempted in the past twenty-four hours, he found that it was taking much longer than he had anticipated. He had to return to the shed for extra hay several times, but luckily the truck toiled along without faltering. Several times during the morning he would have liked to stop for something to eat, but he feared that he might be unable to start the truck again, so he kept working. But surely he had finished now.

'I reckon that must be the last,' he told Charcoal

as he got back into the truck, ready to turn it and drive it back to the shed for the last time.

From the vantage point of the truck he checked the paddocks, just to be sure that he had not missed any of the groups. He spotted one more small bunch of cows down at the river end of the property, just where the front fence began. Well, that would be the last of them anyway, he thought, making sure that a few bales of hay were still left on the truck. He began to drive slowly and carefully across to the cows; then, daringly, since this was his last chance, he put the truck into second gear for a short time as he bumped along.

He was concentrating more on driving the truck than on the small group of animals that he was approaching, so that he did not realise until he had stopped the truck, and distributed the last of the hay across the ground, that all the animals there were not moving quickly across to the feed. One cow, he now saw, was outside the fence. The fence was broken.

Ben sighed. Lunch would have to wait. He had no choice but to switch off the truck's motor, hoping that he would be able to restart it later because he would have to drive it back up to the shed for the night. His first and most urgent job was to bring the errant cow back through the fence, then mend the wire before other cows found the gap. He scrabbled around in the toolbox for pliers. Charcoal whined and pressed his face against the window, so Ben opened the truck door to let him out.

'I suppose you're getting tired of sitting cooped up in there,' he said, adding the warning, 'but don't go near those cows.'

Ben was pleased to see that Charcoal appeared to ignore the animals. He dropped down on to the grass, and lay watching keenly as Ben went across to the fence to inspect the damage. It's just as well that only one cow managed to get outside, the boy thought, because even one will be hard enough to handle. The space through the broken fence was quite small. Still, the hay that he had strewn would be an inducement, of course; he could coax the cow back with that. He noted with relief that the cow was already showing a keen interest in returning.

Ben climbed through the broken wire on to the road. He was puzzled, and uneasy too, although he could not think why. Perhaps it was because the straggler was one of the quiet Jerseys, a placid cow and certainly not given to breaking down fences like this. It was more a follower than a leader. It was odd to find it here in such circumstances. He told himself that was why he felt so disturbed.

He stifled his anxiety and concentrated on driving the cow back through the break in the fence; but the animal had become so edgy because of its separation from the others that he might have found it impossible, had not Charcoal suddenly jumped the fence to stand beside him. The Jersey took one startled look at the dog, then lowered its head meekly and hurried through the gap.

'That was great!' Ben told the dog.

He was glad that he had discovered the cow before it wandered on to the road. Not that there was much traffic about at any time, but stock was always in danger if it strayed. On the thought, Ben lifted his head from the repair job that he was doing on the wire, and looked towards the Mount Everest corner.

He stood transfixed, unable to believe what he could see there. Ambling along, side by side in the centre of the road, like two contented bushwalkers, were Bossy and Star. Ben dropped the pliers and began to run.

'Bossy! Star!' he yelled.

They gave no indication that they had heard, but

kept up their steady walk.

'Bossy!' Ben yelled again as he ran. 'Star!'

His mind was a jumble of calamities, but he tried to keep calm as he puffed along. At least he could see them, that was something. What if they'd got lost? How would he have ever found them again? His father's best cows. Winded, but now much closer to the cows, he stopped to get his breath, prepared to run again.

He heard the tourist coach's horn. For a paralysing moment the sound seemed to be merely a dreadful echo in his head. The tourist coach. He had completely forgotten it. It was not late today. It was on time, bustling down the mountain, and it would turn the Mount Everest corner in a matter of minutes. Bossy and Star were now only fifty metres from the corner. No, less. The coach would hit them. Kill them. And the coach—there'd be a dreadful accident.

Even as the thoughts were churning around in his head, he was running. Even though he knew that he had no hope of reaching the corner in time, he was running. Shouting.

'Get off the road!'

Futile. The cows kept on, walking steadily towards the corner, towards the tourist coach that would turn the corner at any moment. Ben kept on running. The air whooped in his lungs. His mind told him that it was hopeless—useless—but his legs still kept moving, pounding along the road. He began to feel that he must be enclosed within glass, running in a strange slow motion, because everything around him had quickened.

Charcoal raced past him, barking. Ben could no longer see the cows because of the mist over his eyes. He stumbled and nearly fell, then he gave up, exhausted, suddenly unable to move another step. He put his hands to his ears, but he knew that hands could not blot out the sound of the tourist coach when it hit the cows, so he dropped them and shook his head hopelessly, to clear his eyes.

The cows had stopped. As Ben took one more laboured breath, sure that his lungs must burst, he saw Charcoal close to the cows' heels. One bark and the dog had moved the cows over to the side of the road just as the coach swung around the corner. It was done so swiftly and smoothly that the coach did not even have to slacken its speed, and Ben had barely time enough to move to the road's edge himself, before the coach rushed past. He was too spent to raise a hand in response to the driver's cheerful wave.

Ben sagged down, his back against a tree. His heart thumped loudly, and almost in time with the cows' hooves as Charcoal drove them back along the grass at the road's edge. When Charcoal reached Ben, he left the cows for a moment and paused to lick Ben's face, as though to comfort him. Ben gathered him close, careful not to touch the wound on the dog's side. He could not speak, but he felt that Charcoal understood how shaky and unnerved he felt.

Ben had to rest for a time, with Charcoal waiting at his side. The cows stood, two bland delinquents, watching the dog warily, not moving. When Ben's heart stopped its dreadful thumping, and when he felt that his legs would support him, he got to his feet and walked slowly back towards the farm. Charcoal drove the cows ahead, still at the side of the road, and Ben marvelled at the dog's command of them; they were no trouble at all. Once they reached the break in the fence Charcoal merely stood in front of them, indicating that they might go no further, and they swerved tamely aside through the gap. Charcoal followed close behind. The other cows had already finished the hay that Ben had left for them earlier beside the truck.

'You've missed out on that, anyway,' he told Bossy

and Star, with bitter satisfaction. 'Now you can do without.'

Later, however, after he had finished mending the fence, he relented, but only because of the milk production. Using the old broom that they always carried in the truck, he swept the remainder of the hay out of the truck on to the grass. Then, leaving the two cows to shoulder each other aside to get at the scraps, he returned to the truck. This time, Charcoal preferred to ride on the back, and Ben had no fear now that the dog would tease or badger the cows. The truck started easily, otherwise Ben would have left it there in the paddock, for, now that the crisis was over, he was gnawingly hungry again.

He sat with Charcoal in the kitchen. When they had finished eating, he intended to take the dog for a long walk around the farm, to show him the river and the dam. After that, he would take him up to the top of Mount Everest. But first he must let him rest for a while, as the vet had instructed.

Ben's mind was simmering with a new plan. He would ring the owner, and he would ask if he could buy Charcoal. It would be easier than sending him back. Ben had always managed to save some of his pocket money, so he had money in the bank. It would be more than enough to buy Charcoal, because he was little more than a pup. And Charcoal had proved that he would be perfect on the farm; he seemed to know exactly how to handle the cows.

Ben fought down an icy feeling when he remembered how close he had come to leaving the dog locked in the house that morning. He had only taken him in the truck on impulse. What would have happened if Charcoal had not been there to help him?

Charcoal only slept for about an hour, but when he woke he was so refreshed and bright that when Ben took him outside and up to the sheds the dog kept running ahead and stopping to look back impatiently at Ben, urging him to hurry. Ben was delighted.

'I told you that you'd soon be better,' he said.

The vet had been right; rest and reassurance were the best things for Charcoal. Ben took him into the shed with him when he inspected the vat to make sure that the thermostat was operating correctly, and they were just emerging from the shed when Charcoal stopped, his ears pricked. He was gazing intently up towards the road. Ben looked too, to see what had caught his attention. He saw a man standing by the front gate, pulling it open, and behind him a large truck was waiting on the road, ready to be driven through. It was the same truck from which Charcoal's crate had fallen.

He must hide Charcoal before the man saw him. Ben stared desperately around him at the sheds. No, there was nowhere here that he could hide him; none of the sheds had locks, so the driver could open them to search, if he decided to. It would have to be the house; he had no choice. Keeping to the shelter of the orchard he ran in a wide arc around to the back door, Charcoal close beside him. When he reached the door he opened it and called Charcoal inside. Ben knew that they were not safe even yet. What if Charcoal began to bark? It would be impossible to convince the man that Charcoal was not here if he barked.

He raced Charcoal into his bedroom, trying desperately to remember the commands that McGlosker shouted at his dogs. Would Charcoal listen to him? The only thing that Ben could recall was 'stay'. He tried it now.

'Stay!'

Charcoal slid down immediately to crouch on the floor, his head still erect and his bright eyes fixed on Ben's face.

'Stay!' Ben repeated, rather uncertainly, then closed the door.

How could you tell a dog to be quiet before it actually began to bark? How could you make it understand? He had often heard McGlosker quieten his dogs, but only while they were barking. Don't bark, Charcoal, he warned silently, as he began to run again. The man mustn't hear you.

Ben did not open the front door to meet the stranger on the verandah. The cold panic that was coursing through his body had made him cunning. He knew that he must draw the man away. Somehow he must prevent him from knocking on the door, in case Charcoal barked in response. He opened the back door as quietly as he could and slipped around the side of the house, moving as silently as possible, running on the grass in order to muffle the sound. He heard the truck's door slam, and then, hidden by the shrubbery, he watched the stranger walk towards their front verandah. Ben risked moving a few metres further, then crossed over to the path. He stood, now, between the man and his truck.

'Hullo!' he called.

The man spun around, startled. He looked doubtfully at Ben, and then back towards the front door that he had been approaching.

'Hullo!' Ben called again.

But this time he lowered his voice a little, hoping that it would draw the man towards him, to talk. He did not want the man to shout back, though, because it might set Charcoal barking. It was a chance he had to take.

It worked. The man walked back towards him, only a few steps, but it was an advantage nevertheless. Ben let out his breath very slowly and hoped that he did not sound as though he had been running.

'You live here?' the stranger said.

The man's tone was rough, but affable enough although Ben noticed that his glance slid away to inspect the house and its surroundings, and the sheds. Ben stood waiting. Let him ask first, he thought. Don't volunteer anything.

'Your father around?'

Ben felt a little trickle of anxiety at the question, but he quelled it, telling himself that the man was making a normal enquiry. He tried to imagine that his father was down in the milking sheds as he nodded in their general direction.

'Dad's busy,' he replied guardedly.

The man switched his hard, appraising stare back to the boy so abruptly that Ben stiffened, suddenly afraid. He was alone on the farm, but the man must not discover that. Not this man. He squared his shoulders and stood a little straighter to face the man, registering his frayed jeans and the grubby T-shirt, the frizzy black hair and the hard face.

'Not at school today?'

'No,' Ben said. He had never seen such unpleasant eyes. He thought of the dead snakes on McGlosker's gate. 'No,' he repeated, and then, because he was sure that this man would not know anything about the school, he added, 'we start tomorrow.'

The man was hardly listening to him, his eyes were constantly shifting, scanning the distance, inspecting the machinery, observing the cows that were gathered near the dam. Counting them?

'Can I have a word with your dad?' the man asked abruptly.

Ben's heart thumped. He was not about to admit to this stranger that he was there on the farm alone.

'Dad's really busy,' he said, and his heart thumped again as he saw annoyance flash across the man's face.

'What about your mother, then? Is she in the house?'

'She's up in the paddocks, I think,' Ben said, deliberately vague. 'We're really busy,' he repeated.

Now the man looked impatient, and Ben could see that he was turning some thought over in his mind as he stood there. Ben gave an involuntary shiver, and hoped that the man had not noticed it. I won't give Charcoal up, he thought, he's not fit to travel, not yet. The thought of Charcoal being shut under the tarpaulin again stiffened him. He braced himself, trying to act as confidently as he would genuinely have done if his father had really been down in the milking shed and his mother really up in the paddocks. He saw the man look covertly at his watch. He's in a hurry, the boy realised, and had a flash of inspiration.

'I could run up and get Mum for you, if you like,' he offered. 'It shouldn't take too long. Not more than— ah—ten minutes or so.'

The man snorted. He took a couple of steps in the direction of the milking sheds, and Ben watched him, terrified. If he goes down there and finds there's no one there, what will I tell him then? How could I explain it? What will I do? Would I have time to take Charcoal, and run somewhere and hide? But the man halted to look at his watch again, and he swung back towards Ben.

'Aren't you the kid I saw the day before yesterday, on the top of that hill over there?'

Ben shrugged. 'Probably.'

'Didn't you whistle me?'

Ben hesitated, trying to keep his face blank. 'I might have. Probably. I usually whistle the cars because we don't get many along here.'

The stranger looked hard at him, and again Ben was reminded of McGlosker's snakes.

'D' you keep any dogs here?'

'Dogs?' Ben tried to look both foolish and bewildered, and by the look of impatience on the man's face, he knew that he had succeeded. He looked around him, inviting the man to look with him, to see for himself that there were none. 'Dogs? No.'

'None at all?'

'No.' Ben thought that he could be allowed a question, so he tried a puzzled, 'Why?'

'Well—I've lost one.'

'Lost a dog?' Ben looked cautiously at the truck. 'Out of your truck, d' you mean?'

The man snorted again. This time he did not answer, but began to walk towards the truck, checking his watch as he went. Silently, Ben urged him on his way. Then, abruptly, the man stopped in midstride, his gaze riveted on the ground in front of him. Ben saw them too, and his heart plunged. Charcoal's paw marks were clearly outlined in the mud beside the drive. The man swung round on Ben, his face ugly with suspicion, and Ben, his body stiff with fright, tried to keep his face impassive.

'I thought you said you didn't have any dogs here,' the man said.

'No, we haven't,' Ben said. 'We don't—we don't really need dogs here, 'cause Dad always uses his motorbike.'

Ben's father had often told him that, and now the sentence rose out of his mind, as though it had been waiting there, ready for just this emergency. The man stared at him, and then down at the tracks again. He half squatted so that he could examine them more closely. Ben felt as though they had been made in quicksand, and he would drown in them. If Charcoal barked now, what could he do?

S p r u n g !

The paw marks. Ben tried to think. How could he explain them when they were obviously so freshly made? Could he say that Charcoal had actually come here to the farm, and then gone away? That he'd chased him away? But how had Charcoal got out of the crate?

'Mr McGlosker –' Ben stopped. His voice sounded so strange and so alien to his ears that he took a deep breath and began again, this time speaking a little louder. 'Mr McGlosker has dogs. He's got sheep, you see, so he keeps a couple of sheepdogs over there on his farm.' At least he had drawn the man's eyes away from Charcoal's tracks. 'He comes here with his dogs sometimes, to see my father.'

'Where does he live, this McGlosker?' The man's face had cleared a little.

'He's got the next place.' Ben pointed down past the truck. 'You can see his sheep over there, on the hill.'

The man nodded. He climbed back into his truck and reversed it too fast, scraping its side against a tree, then he turned with a loud clash of gears and sped up the long drive to the gate. He had not closed the gate when he came through it earlier, and he did not stop to close it now. Ben watched with disgust as the truck raced up the road in the direction of McGlosker's farm.

Ben walked up to the gate and swung it shut, his

mind busy counting the number of days since McGlosker had called. The driver had gone up to ask McGlosker. What a fuss about a dog. Would McGlosker tell the man that he had not visited them for a least a week? If he did, would the driver come back to check the tracks again? Yet McGlosker would confirm that Ben and his father kept no dogs on their property, wouldn't he, and that was exactly what Ben had told the man. Alternating between hope and despair, Ben went back to the house. He looked very closely at Charcoal's paw marks when he reached them, and he even considered getting a rake from the shed to smooth them over. He decided against that, however, because it would look too suspicious if the man came back.

When Ben returned he was astonished to find Charcoal still waiting, still crouching and watching the door. The boy patted him warmly.

'I can't take you outside after all,' he said. 'It's too dangerous.'

But just a little later he saw the truck returning from McGlosker's farm, thundering along at top speed, and as far as he could tell, the driver did not even look in their direction.

The man had gone. Charcoal was safe. Even though Ben reassured himself about that repeatedly, he took Charcoal for his walk down to that part of the river that was furthest from the road. Charcoal needed to be exercised, so they must walk together, and Ben knew that it would be easier to spot the truck from down by the river, should the man return. In such a case, Ben planned to stay hidden amongst the trees. When they reached the fence that bordered the river he scrambled through the wire with the dog, and then sat down in the shade of a gum tree to watch the water.

Next to Mount Everest, this was his favourite place. From here you could trace the route that the river took, by charting the river red gums that accompanied it like a column of green-cloaked pilgrims trudging faithfully on each side of the river no matter where it turned and twisted. Although it had been known to flood, Ben could not remember it happening, but his father had often pointed out the debris which was still lodged high in some of the trees.

The river was not very wide at this point, and Ben could easily hit the trees opposite with stones when he wanted to, but the banks were very steep and the bushes and trees were thick. Manna gums and gully gums grew here amongst the river red gums so that it was a haven for birds. Ben knew that a family of rainbow lorikeets nested close by, but that it would be late afternoon before they would emerge to feed and chatter, vivid jewels darting amongst the trees as they searched for nectar.

Charcoal lay beside Ben with his head on the boy's knee, resting. Ben wished that he had thought to bring his fishing rod, but instead, he watched the two black swans that had taken up residence on the river, to wait out their moulting period. When that was completed, they would probably fly away, at least for a while. In sharp contrast to the black swans, a snow-white egret walked delicately on tendril legs, luminous against the dark green reeds that edged the river, pausing at intervals to dip its bill into the water.

While he sat watching the swans as they circled languidly, he composed a letter in his mind to Emu Creek. He had decided that a letter would be more satisfactory than a telephone call, for if he rang he might be asked to return Charcoal immediately, perhaps even give him to the truck driver at once. On the other hand, if he wrote a letter Ben thought that he would have a chance to explain fully about the accident, and exactly what had happened. He would also offer to buy

65

Charcoal, and that would save everyone the trouble of organising his return; he could stay with Ben.

Ben assured himself that nobody else would be worrying about the dog, for he had a shrewd idea that the driver would not have reported Charcoal's disappearance yet. He thought back over the days as he stroked Charcoal's head. Sunday, Monday, and today. It was hard to remember what their farm had been like before Charcoal had arrived. He wondered briefly what his mother and father would say, but then he tucked that little worry firmly away, for he was sure that they would not mind if he spent his pocket money on a dog, especially one as useful as Charcoal would be. McGlosker was always telling his father that he should get himself a dog.

Now Ben was hungry again. He would have a huge afternoon tea so that he would not feel as hungry as he usually did when he was milking. As he and Charcoal walked back from the river he was busily planning that he would get some extra food out of the freezer too, ready to heat for dinner.

When he was halfway back he saw McGlosker's utility truck parked near the house, so he hurried a little, but not so fast that he would tire Charcoal. McGlosker must have been out when the truck driver called on him. McGlosker's two sheepdogs were on the back of the truck, and they began to bark when Ben was still a fair way off because they caught sight of Charcoal, a strange dog. Charcoal walked a little straighter when the barking began. He pricked his ears, and looked up at Ben as though for instructions. But, when the boy shook his head, the dog relaxed and sauntered along with him as before.

Like most farmers in the area, McGlosker drove a small, crumpled utility truck, the tray piled with coils of fencing wire, rusting tools and bags of feed for the sheep. Wherever he drove, and at whatever speed, his two sheepdogs balanced happily on the back amongst the jumble. Now, they barked even louder as Ben neared them; first down at Ben in their usual fashion, to show that they recognised him; then even more clamorously at the strange dog.

McGlosker was a very tall, pole-thin man, with hair and moustache the same sandy colour as his truck. He stood, unmoving, beside the truck as Ben approached. The boy began to feel uneasy the nearer he came, for he could not fail to see an expression on McGlosker's face – an unexpected expression – of surprise, and something else. Was it disappointment? Why?

'A new dog?' McGlosker asked, but not in his usual, friendly way.

Ben nodded, awkwardly. McGlosker turned and shouted at his dogs to quieten them.

'A sheepdog, eh?'

Ben nodded again. Although McGlosker's voice was as dry and crisp as always, his tone was different. It occurred to Ben that he had heard his father say that McGlosker had been a colonel during the war, although he did not know why he should recall that now, unless it was because McGlosker was standing very stiff and straight and looking down at him very closely. He did not look pleased at all. Something's wrong, the boy thought.

'You're not at school I see, Ben. I saw you going for the bus yesterday. Did you manage to catch it?'

Ben swallowed hard. 'No,' he admitted. 'I missed it.' I would have caught it, though, if your sheep hadn't been all over the road, he added – but silently.

'You should have been up earlier, if you had a bus to catch.'

This was so unfair, when he remembered his efforts on Monday morning, that Ben had to bite back very hard on the remark that he wanted to make. Instead, he bent down and stroked Charcoal's head. When he looked up, he caught that strange, unfriendly look on McGlosker's face again.

'Did you miss the bus again this morning?'

Ben nodded because he could think of no other response. McGlosker would have been a pretty tough colonel, he thought. The man's coldness was now so obvious that Ben felt tongue-tied and miserable. McGlosker waited for a moment as though expecting something more, but when Ben remained silent, he said abruptly, looking down at Charcoal again, 'I think I'd better have a word with your dad while I'm here. Is he down in the shed?'

'No, Mr McGlosker.'

'Out, is he? When will he be back?'

'I don't know, Mr McGlosker,' Ben said. Perhaps he had misunderstood, and it was his father who had offended their neighbour.

'You don't know?' McGlosker gave Ben another of those unfamiliar stares. 'Mother home, then?'

'No. She's with Dad.'

Would he mention his father's accident? Surely there was no harm in telling a neighbour, although now Ben was quite glad that he had been unable to raise McGlosker to ask for his help. McGlosker turned to his utility and got in, and the dogs stood on the back of the truck, ready to go, tails wagging furiously now.

'Tell them that I'll come over after dinner, then,' McGlosker called back to the boy.

'They won't be home,' Ben told him.

McGlosker had already started the car, but now he turned the motor off and stared at Ben, but this time with a faint softening in his expression.

'Is anything wrong, Ben?'

Ben nodded. 'Dad's in the hospital, Mr McGlosker,

and Mum's gone with him. Dad had an accident with the power saw. His arm. He's had to have an operation on it.' It was a relief to tell someone at last, even if it was such bad news.

'Well!' Then, more thoughtfully, 'Well!'

McGlosker got out of his car again and stood, gazing over at the cattle, but not in the hard, calculating way that the truck driver had stared earlier. 'I'm really sorry to hear that, Ben.' He looked a little less like an army colonel, Ben was pleased to see. 'Went to the hospital this morning, did he?'

'No, on Sunday.'

'Two days ago!'

McGlosker's voice was so sharp that the two dogs started to bark again, almost as though McGlosker had jabbed them. He roared over his shoulder, 'Be quiet, there!' He looked towards the sheds. 'Who've you got here, helping you? The Carters?'

'No. I rang them like Dad told me to, but they were both down with flu, or something. I guess that they can hardly manage their own place at the moment.'

'They'd have their son, he'd have come over to help,' McGlosker said, rather absently. 'But you—who've you managed to get hold of?'

'No one.'

'But what about the herd?' McGlosker asked. He was looking faintly alarmed. 'And your milk contract? Whatever will your parents think when they come back and find the place in a mess and the cows gone dry.'

'Everything's fine,' Ben told him indignantly. 'I've milked them, and everything's all right.'

'Milked the cows yourself, did you?' McGlosker looked around, and then, a short pause later, 'All of them?'

Ben wondered if Bossy's and Star's reputations could be well known. 'Yes. All of them.'

69

'And you've managed to cover your milk contract.'

'Yes.' Ben could not help it if he sounded proud.

'Mmm.' McGlosker stood, drumming his fingers on the car roof, his eyes fixed on Charcoal again, but this time more thoughtfully.

'If you've got a message for Dad, I could tell Mum when she rings,' Ben offered after a moment, feeling awkward about McGlosker's silence. 'She'll be ringing me later, I'm sure.'

'No, no,' McGlosker said. He was obviously thinking of something else, and trying to make up his mind. He shifted his gaze from the dog back to Ben.

'I've had a visit from a man today,' he said, and it seemed to Ben that he was picking his words with great care. 'This fellow told me that he had a bit of bad luck. He stopped for lunch along the road here, and afterwards he went for a bit of a stroll to have a rest from the driving. He wasn't away long, but—ah—someone broke into his vehicle while he was gone and stole something.'

A pause, while Ben looked back at him, bewildered but sure that there must be a point to the story, and that McGlosker would get to it eventually.

'Yes,' repeated McGlosker; his hard stare had returned. 'He stole something.'

Ben waited. Why did McGlosker look so disapprovingly at him? And why should he be so interested in a theft?

'Ah, well,' McGlosker said, becoming very brisk, and making for his utility again. 'Perhaps it'd be better if we look into that a bit later, eh? You've got enough to handle here, at the moment. I'll wait till your parents get back. I promised this driver that I'd keep a lookout for his—his property.'

He had restarted the utility and was turning it before any of his words made sense to Ben. As they gradually seeped through, he stood, appalled, then he chased the utility, catching up with it just as it had finished its turn. He banged on its roof as hard as he could, and McGlosker looked back out of the window, surprised.

'Mr McGlosker! Mr McGlosker!' Ben yelled.

Pandemonium! McGlosker's two dogs barked even more furiously than they had earlier, and this time Charcoal joined in. McGlosker wound down his window, took another look at Ben's indignant face, then cut the engine once again. He got out and quietened the dogs, but he said nothing to Ben until silence reigned, then he nodded to the boy to speak.

'Mr McGlosker!' Ben had found it hard enough to contain his fury as he waited for the dogs to stop barking, and now he was too incensed to care if he sounded rude. 'That wasn't how it happened, not at all. That awful man – that truckie – he never even stopped. As a matter of fact, he was going so fast that he nearly ran off the road.'

'The truck didn't stop? You didn't break into it?'

'Break into his truck!' Ben repeated, even more enraged at the enormity of the suggestion. 'At that speed? I'm not Superman! He came along the road here so fast that he took the corner up there – you know that turn at the bottom of Mount – at the bottom of that big hill – that very sharp corner? Well, he nearly went clean off the road there.'

Ben could see that he was talking too fast, and not telling the story clearly, because McGlosker was now looking confused.

'How did he lose his dog, then?'

Ben tried to slow down a little. 'I was up there on the hill, so I saw what happened. The truck came along, and its tarpaulin was all loose.' Break into his truck, indeed! Ben nearly choked at the thought, but he

71

recovered and continued. 'And when he swung round that corner, the box came off the back.'

'The box?' McGlosker still looked baffled.

'Well, a crate then. The dog was in a crate. A wooden one. And that's what happened. The dog fell off the back of the truck.'

'Fell off the back of the truck?' McGlosker repeated rather faintly.

In all the times that McGlosker had visited his father, Ben had never heard the man laugh. He had not expected him to laugh now, so that he stood, astonished at first, as McGlosker threw back his head, and laughed and laughed until tears rolled down his face, and the dogs began to bark again. But his laugh was so infectious that Ben began to laugh too. It felt great.

'Fell off the back of a truck, eh?' McGlosker said at last, wiping his face with a handkerchief. 'If that's not the funniest thing I've ever heard. Quiet, there!' he roared back at his dogs.

'Well, Ben,' he continued after another minute, and his face had become grave again. 'That's certainly not the story that he's telling. I'd better hear the rest of yours, I suppose.'

Ben had had time to sort his thoughts out a little, and so he told the story from the beginning, a little more coherently. 'Then,' he continued, 'I just didn't have any time to think about the crate for a while. I completely forgot it when Dad had the accident. I did the milking on Monday morning, and then I missed the bus, you see.'

At this reminder, McGlosker looked a little embarrassed, but he said nothing and Ben proceeded.

'So I had to come back home. That's when I remembered about the truck, so I went up the road to have a look for the crate. If it was still there, I thought

I might be able to find out who it belonged to and let them know, so that they could come and collect it.'

McGlosker nodded, and Ben looked down at Charcoal, remembering that first whimper that he had heard, and the little, dark huddle at the back of the box. And the blood. He took a deep breath so that his voice would stop trembling, and McGlosker would not notice how much it upset him to remember.

'I didn't have a clue what was in it; it'd slid right down off the road into the bracken, and it was pretty dark anyway, in the trees there. Then, I looked through this little window at the side, and I saw him, all huddled up.' Ben swallowed hard. 'I managed to get him out though, and there was—there was this awful cut, there, on his side. So I called the vet, and he came, and he told me that the dog was OK but he'd need a lot of rest and care, because he'd had such a fright.'

He stopped. McGlosker's gaze was fixed intently on Ben's face, and the boy recalled, quite abruptly and unexpectedly, that his father had once told him that McGlosker's one passion in life was his sheepdogs.

'And, then?' McGlosker prompted.

'He was shocked, I guess, because he slept and slept. He'd been left there all Sunday night, you see, after he was hurt. And then that truck driver came here, and started asking questions. But I just couldn't give him up, Mr McGlosker. I couldn't. He'd have just put him in another of those crates, straight away, and Charcoal's not fit enough. I couldn't let him know that Charcoal was here.'

His voice wobbled again, so he stopped. McGlosker looked down at Charcoal, and then at his own dogs. He stood silent. What'll I do? the boy wondered, as he waited. If he says I must give Charcoal back, well, I can't. But what will I do?

McGlosker bent down to examine Charcoal's side. He was as gentle and thorough as the vet had been. He looked up at Ben.

'It was Sunday, you say, when the truck lost its load.'

'Sunday afternoon.'

'And when did the driver come back to look for it?'

'Not until after lunch on Monday. And again this afternoon.'

McGlosker's reaction was the same as the vet's had been. 'He didn't check the dog on Sunday night, then. And the crate. How was it that the driver didn't find the crate, when you managed to?'

Ben hesitated, but he knew that it would do no good to tell lies about what had happened. 'I took it to pieces, and hid it. Oh, I kept a couple of things—the owner's name, so I could let him know later. And the dog's name too. The man couldn't find it.'

If Ben's villainy shocked him, McGlosker gave no sign. He was stroking Charcoal's head now. 'So you kept the owner's name,' he said thoughtfully. He raised one hand and Charcoal responded by sitting down immediately. McGlosker looked delighted.

'It's inside, in the kitchen,' Ben volunteered. 'Could you—would you like to come and have a look at it?'

Ben led McGlosker through to the kitchen, proud that it still looked quite tidy, and took the pieces of wood that he had preserved and placed them on the table. McGlosker turned them over in his hands, reading.

'An Emu Creek dog, eh?' he murmured. 'Imagine that, now. I see there's this other address too, that'd be where they were sending the dog. Lucky fellow, to be getting an Emu Creek sheepdog. I guess, though, you'd better advise them at Emu Creek, because it's their responsibility.' When Ben remained silent, he eyed him

74

sharply. 'You'll have to advise them, Ben.'

Ben nodded, reluctantly, not sure if this was the time to tell the man that he intended to buy the dog.

McGlosker was examining the third piece of wood. 'I see that they called him Charcoal. And he's not quite fully grown. Mmm, it'd be a real setback to a young dog to have an accident like that.' He put the pieces back on the table. 'I can understand why that fellow would invent a story like he did. He had a contract to deliver the dog, and he lost the animal through negligence, so he'd have a lot of explaining to do. A story of theft would sound better—more convincing.' He gave a snort of disgust. 'With the heartrending story that he gave me, I was quite convinced that it was his own dog that he'd lost.'

And you thought that I'd stolen him, Ben thought, still not forgiving him.

'I'm glad that you saved the little fellow,' McGlosker said. 'I've got a lot of sympathy for anyone who's lost a dog, you know, and that driver made it sound very plausible. It looked bad, too, when I got here and found that you had a sheepdog when I knew that your dad hasn't got one.'

Ben nodded unwillingly. Yes, he could see now how it must have looked to McGlosker.

'The thing that puzzles me,' McGlosker continued, 'is why on earth Emu Creek would entrust a dog of theirs to that sort of carrier. It's quite incredible.' He shrugged his shoulders, then said more briskly, 'How about bringing Charcoal over to my place now, and see how he works the sheep?'

It was the last thing that he had expected, and Ben hardly knew how to answer him. Work McGlosker's sheep? He'd love to see Charcoal do that, but he still had the evening's milking to do. More important, though, was Charcoal well enough to work? He looked down at the dog doubtfully. McGlosker had been watching his face.

'Charcoal's quite fit enough to do some light work. In fact, a bit of a run with the sheep will do him a lot of good, because it's the sort of exercise that he's used to; he loves it. And don't worry, we won't overwork him.' Then, as Ben still looked anxious, he added, 'And don't worry about the milking, either. When we come back, I'll be glad to give you a hand with it. I only wish that I'd known about your dad's accident before this, because I'd have been over to help you before.'

'OK,' Ben nodded, although his vision of the large afternoon tea that he had promised himself receded as he spoke. It couldn't be helped, and it would be great not to have to do all the milking by himself.

'Jump in,' said McGlosker.

Ben sat next to McGlosker in the utility as he started the engine for the third time in the past thirty minutes, and Charcoal sat on the seat next to the window. McGlosker drove carefully over the cattlegrid and up to the front gate, and Ben jumped out to open it, then close it as soon as the utility had driven through.

'One day someone will invent a gate that opens and shuts automatically,' McGlosker commented as Ben climbed back into the utility. 'It's one thing that I haven't been able to train my dogs to do for me.'

They drove over the small bridge that crossed the river, and along the road until they reached McGlosker's property. There, McGlosker parked the utility beside a large, open shed.

'Just wait there for a moment, Ben,' he said. 'I'll have a word with my wife.'

Ben watched McGlosker vanish into the house. 'We're lucky that he likes sheepdogs, Charcoal,' he told the dog beside him. He noticed how alert Charcoal had become since he had first sighted the sheep that grazed in the paddocks around the McGloskers' farmhouse.

'I guess you'd rather live on a sheep station than on a dairy farm, Charcoal, but you're not going to miss sheep all that much if Mr McGlosker will let you come over here sometimes.'

McGlosker came back shortly and opened the door of the utility, indicating that they were to get out. 'Come along,' he said.

Mrs McGlosker met them at the door. She was an artist. Some of her paintings of Coonara hung in the National Gallery, and Ben had often admired them there when the school visited the gallery. She had evidently been painting because an easel and canvas were still set up at the far end of the long kitchen, where huge windows looked towards a clump of paperbark trees outside. White, fluffy blossoms, like fresh snow, crowned each tree.

'They're late flowering this year,' she told Ben, seeing that he had stopped, absorbed by the view. 'But the blossoms are holding well.' She indicated the table. 'Just sit there, Ben, we're going to have something to eat first.'

Ben brightened. Not only could Mrs McGlosker paint, but she could cook, too. She won prizes at the Sydney show for her cooking. Every year. He watched appreciatively as she darted between cake tins and the refrigerator, and the table top gradually disappeared under the plates that she set on it. Scones. Cakes. A cream sponge.

'Help yourself, Ben,' Mrs McGlosker said.

Ben hesitated. McGlosker, sitting opposite, pushed a plate towards him. Ben's hand hovered over a large piece of chocolate sponge. He caught Mrs McGlosker's nod, so he took the sponge and began to eat.

'I'm so sorry to hear about your father,' she told

him. 'But I believe that you're managing very well on your own, though.'

Ben nodded, pleased, his mouth full. He wondered if he would be allowed another piece. McGlosker and his wife were buttering scones.

'I'm going to go back with Ben to help him with the milking,' McGlosker said. She nodded. She also pushed the plate of chocolate sponge closer to Ben.

'Do have some more of this sponge, Ben. We'll never be able to eat it on our own, you know.'

Ben started on another piece. It would be dreadful to throw chocolate sponge out, especially chocolate sponge as nice as this one.

'Ben is caring for a sheepdog,' McGlosker said. 'It was injured in an accident, but not badly, thank goodness. We've brought him over here to give him a little bit of light exercise, haven't we, Ben?' He looked across at his wife. 'When we have more time, I'll fill you in about where the dog came from.'

'I should imagine that it'd concern that man who called in earlier,' she said shrewdly. 'He shouldn't be driving a truck around this part of the country.'

'There's a lot of things he shouldn't be doing,' McGlosker said. 'He left our gate wide open,' he told Ben.

'Ours, too,' Ben said, but his voice was rather muffled because of his third piece of chocolate sponge.

A turn
for the worse

When they had finished they left Mrs McGlosker to resume her painting, and went outside. McGlosker took his own dogs into the shed, settled them in a corner, and told them to stay there.

'Not that they couldn't learn a thing or two from your dog,' he told Ben. 'But I'd like to see how Charcoal works on his own.'

Ben was happily conscious of McGlosker's use of the words 'your dog'. I'll tell him, presently, that I'm going to buy Charcoal, he decided. I reckon he'll be pleased.

'We'll go up to the top paddocks, so in you get again, you two,' McGlosker said, indicating the utility, and when they were settled, he said, 'Now we can begin.' He scanned his paddocks as though for inspiration, then pointed. 'That small mob of sheep up there, in the far paddock. See them there?'

Ben nodded. There were about fifty sheep in the group that McGlosker was indicating. They drove a little closer to them, then stopped.

'This'll do nicely. We'll have a good view and Charcoal hasn't very far to run from here. I promised you that I wouldn't overwork him, remember? Now then, we'll send Charcoal up to that lot, and get him to drive them through that open gate over on the left, into the smaller paddock.'

'But will he know what you want him to do?'

'This dog will,' McGlosker replied with certainty. 'There's a couple of troublemakers in the mob of sheep – we have our Bossy and our Star too, you know – sheep that never want to go where you want them to go.'

So McGlosker knows that we have a couple of cows at our place that are hard to handle, Ben thought, and he knows that I managed to milk them. He sat a little straighter in the car.

'When they brought sheep out to Australia in the early days,' McGlosker said, 'they had shepherds watching them, just like they'd had back in England, and in Scotland. The shepherds here, though, were usually convicts. Sometimes they were ticket-of-leave men – those who'd already served part of their sentences. I think that shepherding in Australia in those days must have been as bad as any other punishment – worse, perhaps. Do you know, Ben,' he said, turning to the boy, 'there'd be a group of three shepherds set up in the middle of nowhere. Hundreds of miles, often, from any other settlers.'

He shook his head. 'They had only a small hut of wood and bark for shelter. Dreadful things, those huts – I've seen one or two that've survived – stifling in summer, freezing in winter.'

'Some of them were killed by the Aborigines,' Ben volunteered.

'Yes, they had no protection. Two of the group had to follow the sheep around all day, and the other one had to remain to guard the hut, and shift the sheep pens, and cook. And, on top of that, he had to watch the sheep at night. Goodness knows when he slept – probably when he was supposed to be guarding the sheep, I suppose.'

Ben grinned. Milking cows twice a day did not seem quite so bad. He knew most of what McGlosker was telling him because it had been discussed in the history class last year; but it seemed quite different now, to think about it while you were actually watching sheep.

'They don't use shepherds now,' he said. 'Why did they stop?'

'Oh, there were a few reasons. After a while the squatters found that it wasn't necessary to watch the sheep so closely, as long as there was someone around to help at lambing time. And transportation declined, so the supply of convicts dried up. The squatters couldn't get free men to live in such dreadful isolation. And fencing improved, that would've helped. But I guess the main reason was the gold. Once gold had been discovered, I'm sure that no one would sit around watching a mob of sheep, day and night, when there might be a fortune waiting to be picked up just the other side of the mountains.'

I'd have left to search for the gold, Ben thought. 'But wouldn't the convicts be caught, and sent back?' he asked.

'I'm sure that would've happened at first, when there weren't many settlers here, but then thousands of new people arrived from overseas and trekked up to the goldfields the minute they got off the ships. Whole ships' crews deserted, you remember. So, by that time, missing shepherds would've been much harder to find. You can easily lose yourself in a crowd, can't you?'

'And what about the sheep?' Ben was watching Charcoal who was staring, unblinking, at the sheep.

'Conditions were quite different here, and I suppose that the squatters learned from experience. Eventually. It didn't hurt the sheep if they weren't watched, in fact they seemed to do better. Perhaps they liked our open spaces? Anyway, some of those squatters made more money from the sheep than the miners did, who were digging for gold.'

'Did they have dogs in those days? Sheepdogs, I mean.' Ben wondered how he could ever have thought that McGlosker was a quiet man, with very little to say about anything.

'Dogs? Yes. They began with the long-haired sheepdogs that they'd brought with them from Scotland. Collies. You've seen them, lovely dogs they are too. After a while, they bred a smooth-haired dog, like Charcoal here. The kelpie. Enthusiastic, wonderful endurance. Fast. And the short coat was an improvement because of our hotter climate.'

Ben touched Charcoal's coat; he could feel it warm under his hand. 'He's a lovely colour,' he said proudly.

McGlosker nodded. 'You get a lot of colours with kelpies — black, tan, red, or a mix of those. Smoke-blue, even.' He stopped to look at Charcoal, and smiled across at Ben. 'D' you know what kelpie means, Ben?' And, as Ben shook his head, McGlosker said, 'Water-devil. A mature kelpie is about — ah, let me think now — about fifty-one centimetres tall, so Charcoal's not quite fully grown yet. A good kelpie can do the work of three men out in the paddocks, and he loves work. That's why I'm sure that Charcoal's going to enjoy this.'

Charcoal had been sitting, listening as though he knew exactly what McGlosker was saying. Ben noticed that his gaze was still fixed on the sheep.

'Look at him,' McGlosker said happily. 'He's counted those sheep already, I'll bet. He's probably worked out by now exactly what we want him to do, and he's just waiting for us to give him the go-ahead.'

He opened the door of the utility and Charcoal jumped down on to the grass, then, not pausing for instructions, he raced up to the sheep.

82

'Not much wrong with him now, is there?' McGlosker observed.

The sheep saw Charcoal coming. The mob swayed a little, and crowded together, and some of the sheep at the edge of the mob turned to face the dog.

'Now, watch him drive them.' As McGlosker spoke, the sheep began to stream towards the gate. 'He doesn't force them, see? They're moving fast because they're afraid of him, and want to get away from him. But he doesn't get so close to them that they'll panic and do silly things, and hurt themselves. A good dog like Charcoal makes sure that they move in the right direction simply by standing in the right place himself.'

'It looks awfully easy,' Ben said. He was almost disappointed.

McGlosker laughed. 'It's a lot harder than it looks, believe me. Charcoal makes it look easy only because he's an expert. If any dog but a good sheepdog approached those sheep, they'd break and go in all directions. You'd waste a lot of time getting them together again. Don't forget that Charcoal has to anticipate what the sheep are going to do; he has to think for them. Like when you're playing tennis and you have to guess where the ball is going to bounce when it comes back to you, so that you're there, ahead of it.'

One of the sheep had baulked at the gate. It turned to face Charcoal and stood, obstinate.

'That's one of our problem sheep,' said McGlosker. 'Let's see how Charcoal handles him.'

Two of the other sheep now slowed uncertainly, and stopped. Charcoal and the first rebel sheep faced each other, heads close together, for a count of about six seconds, then Ben heard Charcoal bark once, sharply. The sheep ducked its head, turned quickly and sped through the gate almost at a gallop, with the other waverers hurrying behind it. Charcoal dropped down on to the grass and remained where he was, watching the sheep.

'See that, Ben?' asked McGlosker unnecessarily. 'That's what we call "eye". The dog almost mesmerises the sheep—forces it to obey by sheer willpower. He doesn't need to bite if he can do that, and a good kelpie doesn't bite. If you have valuable sheep you need a dog that'll treat them carefully. And Charcoal knew just when to bark to make the point that he was boss. Did you notice? See him there now, perfectly still. The sheep know that he's there, and Charcoal knows that he'll make them nervous if he moves around, so he just lies there, making sure that they don't try to come back through the gate.' McGlosker sighed. 'A beautiful worker. What a pity we won't see him work when he's fully grown.'

Perhaps now was the time to tell him. 'Mr McGlosker,' Ben began. He stopped, wondering how best to put it, because he felt that McGlosker's approval and help might be important. 'D' you think that I could buy Charcoal?'

He was disturbed by McGlosker's look of complete astonishment, and even more shaken by the man's obvious alarm. McGlosker began to speak, but Ben hurried on. 'I've got a bit of money, I've been saving some of my pocket money for ages, and I'm sure that Dad won't mind me having a dog.' Then, because McGlosker was looking even more troubled, Ben played what he hoped would be his trump card. 'It'll save all the fuss of sending him away and upsetting him again.'

McGlosker seemed to be struggling to find words, and Ben's heart fell. It did not look as though he was going to get the support that he had hoped for, and that was strange because he had expected that McGlosker would be glad if he bought him, and Charcoal stayed.

'I'll look after him, you know,' he assured the silent

man beside him. 'And any time that he gets tired of herding our cows, well, perhaps you won't mind if he comes over here sometimes and helps with your sheep.' There! If Charcoal was as good as McGlosker said, surely now he would be pleased.

'You've grown very fond of that dog, haven't you?' McGlosker asked. It was a statement, rather than a question, and he sounded sad, as though he was sorry about it. Ben could not understand it. He had thought that McGlosker would have encouraged him, and been glad that he wanted to keep Charcoal.

'He's an Emu Creek sheepdog,' McGlosker said, as though he was explaining something. Then, as Ben looked at him blankly, the man sighed, began to speak, stopped, and then said, 'Well, I told you we won't overwork him, so whistle him back now, Ben.'

Complete silence. A little surprised by Ben's lack of response, McGlosker turned to look at him. Ben was sitting bolt upright, white-faced, his gaze riveted on the rear-vision mirror. Framed in it at a distance lay the farmhouse, tranquil in the late sunshine, fringed by the white-capped paperbark trees. Beside the farmhouse a vehicle had just pulled to a halt – the truck with the green tarpaulin. McGlosker, now intent on the mirror's image also, spoke very fast; urgently.

'There's no need for you to worry, Ben.' As Ben made an instinctive movement towards the car door he added sharply, 'No, stay here, Ben. It'll be better if he doesn't see you here. My wife'll keep him talking while I decide what to do. She'll know that we'll spot him from here, and she won't tell him anything, never fear.'

Ben sat perfectly still, but his hand remained white-clenched on the door handle. He stared at Charcoal, crouched there, watching the sheep. Why ever had they come here to McGlosker's farm? Back home he would have known places that he could have escaped to – places that the truck driver would never have found. But here? Would he have time to grab Charcoal and run? But where? The river? He looked across at the line of trees that marked where the river crossed McGlosker's paddocks. Could he reach it with Charcoal before he was caught?

'Don't worry, Ben,' McGlosker said, his voice so quiet and assured that Ben relaxed just a little, although he still gripped the utility's door handle. 'It'll be all right. I have no intention of letting that fellow know that Charcoal is here. He has no idea how to look after a beautiful animal like this one.'

'But he'll see him,' Ben said desperately. At that moment, Charcoal looked as large as an elephant, there on the grass. 'Look, he can see him now.' Indeed, the man was looking in their direction.

'Do you really think that a fellow like that would know one sheepdog from another?' McGlosker asked drily. 'He already knows that I keep sheepdogs, remember.' He turned the key in the ignition and started the car. 'We'll leave Charcoal here to guard the sheep— he won't move until we tell him—and I'll go back and talk to the driver to see what he's up to this time.'

He drove back towards the farmhouse and parked a short distance from where the truck had stopped. 'Now, stay here and wait, Ben. I'll be back in a minute.' His eyes were intent on the boy's worried face as he added, 'Ben, trust me. Remember, I'm not giving Charcoal back to him.'

Ben released the door handle at last and sat back on the seat, waiting, trying to slow his racing heart. He watched McGlosker walk to meet the driver. To Ben's surprise, they talked only briefly, then the driver handed McGlosker a small card and returned to his truck. McGlosker came back to where Ben was waiting.

'I told him to shut that gate, or there'll be trouble,' was all he said at first, before he got back into the utility.

He looked very grave and anxious now, and Ben wondered what the driver could have said in so short a time to worry him. McGlosker held the card that the driver had given him, but Ben was not able to see what was printed on it.

'We'll go back and collect Charcoal now,' McGlosker said.

He drove back to where Charcoal was waiting, and leaned over to open the door of the utility. 'Hop in, Charcoal,' he told the dog, then turning to Ben, 'I'll take you both back home now, and we'll do something about that milking.'

He did not start his car immediately, however, but sat there, looking at Charcoal. After a pause he took out the card that he had put away in his pocket a few minutes before.

'There's a bit of a problem, and I suppose that we'd better talk about it,' he said, indicating the card. 'Something has come up that I really hadn't thought about, although I should have. It's important, quite important.'

Ben knew from McGlosker's tone that this would not be good news, so he braced himself as the man continued. 'You see, Ben, it's the insurance.'

'Insurance?' Ben asked, blankly.

McGlosker nodded. 'The truck driver believes that the dog is lost, and we haven't told him otherwise. He's left me his card, here, so that I can advise him if the dog turns up. That driver won't be coming back, he tells me that he's running very late now, and he has to complete his run to Sydney.'

Ben's taut muscles eased. So the truck driver's visit had nothing whatsoever to do with any suspicion that they were harbouring the dog. But wouldn't that be good news, rather than bad? Why should McGlosker be upset about it?

'The dog is insured,' the man explained patiently.

'Charcoal's insured against loss or injury, you see.'

Ben tried very hard to see, because McGlosker obviously expected him to understand, but he could not. What did insurance have to do with them?

'That truck driver,' McGlosker said, even more gently, and now with that earlier sadness, 'he's going to apply to the insurance company – make a claim. And he'll have to advise them as soon as possible. I'm afraid that there's no hope, now, of keeping Charcoal for even an extra day or two. We'll have to let them know that we've found him, right away.'

'Why?' Ben could still see no connection. He put an arm around Charcoal defensively, and the dog dropped his head against Ben's leg and shut his eyes. He knows that he's safe, the boy thought.

'If the insurance company accepts the claim, it will pay the truck driver, or the owner, depending on the contract.'

'Insurance company?' Ben had never heard anything so stupid, but he said it very quietly, because Charcoal was asleep. 'Insurance? For a dog?'

Eyes downcast, McGlosker flicked the card backwards and forwards against his thumb, as though undecided, then he lifted his gaze to Ben's face.

'Ben,' he said, 'Charcoal's a very valuable dog. Emu Creek dogs sell for an average of one thousand dollars.'

McGlosker turned the key in the ignition and they drove off. Ben did not remember, later, anything about the silent drive home, nor did he recall opening and shutting the gates, although he felt that he must have done so. As though in a dream, he heard McGlosker speak at last.

'Look, Ben! Your car is back. Your mum and dad are home.'

All hope lost —
and found

'It was such a stupid thing to do.'

His father had been telling McGlosker about his accident, and Ben sat watching, but only half listening. He had left Charcoal outside on the verandah, so that his parents had not yet seen the dog, and had not therefore asked questions about him. Ben's mind seemed to be vibrating still with McGlosker's words, but now his apathy was giving way to anger. He should have known how it would be. It always happened. The minute that adults knew about anything at all, they interfered so that it all became impossible. One thousand dollars. How could a dog cost so much money? McGlosker must be wrong.

'I suppose that at least I'm an example to Ben,' his father continued, easing his bandaged arm in its sling. 'A very bad example—how one should not use power tools. I was daydreaming while I worked, you see, and instead of holding the saw with both hands, I left one hand on the timber while I was cutting it. And look what happened to me. Remember it, Ben.'

'I will.'

'We drove down to the hospital at Coonara first,' his mother said. 'They sent us on to Sydney, because they don't handle microsurgery at Coonara. His hand will be as good as new, you know. It was quite miraculous, what the surgeons did. He has to report to Coonara Hospital each day for a week or so, for follow-up treatment – he'll begin that tomorrow. He wanted to make sure that everything was all right at home first.' She swung around to smile warmly at Ben. 'You didn't tell me when I rang you that Mr McGlosker was helping you here, Ben. I thought you'd asked the Carters.'

'I did,' Ben said. 'Well, I tried, but they were both sick.'

When his father tried to thank McGlosker, the man shook his head. 'No need to thank me. I've only come over to help Ben with the milking now. I didn't even know about your accident until this afternoon, so up till now Ben's managed very well, all by himself.'

Ben scarcely noticed the surprise on his father's face, and he was hardly aware of the warmth of his voice as he praised him. One thousand dollars, Ben was thinking. How does McGlosker know that for sure, anyway? He could be wrong. He must be wrong. He saw the worried look that his mother directed at him. So did McGlosker.

'Ben's been having quite a few adventures while you two have been away,' he explained, an odd note in his voice. 'He'll probably tell you about them later, when he has time.' A pause. 'He found a sheepdog that had been involved in an accident, just up at the corner, and he's been caring for him.'

'A sheepdog?' his father said. He was watching McGlosker very closely, and his mother's attention was fixed on McGlosker too. Ben turned from her to McGlosker just in time to see him shake his head warningly at them both. Ben stood up. He would leave them to discuss him. He had to think.

'I'll go out and get the shed ready,' he said, addressing the space between McGlosker and his father.

Charcoal followed him, and sat watching while the

boy prepared the machinery, making everything ready for the milking. Ben worked quickly, mechanically, forgetting nothing. He was planning what he would do. I've got to find a way, he thought. McGlosker joined him.

'I've told your parents that they can go and have a rest while we're doing the milking.' McGlosker was very matter-of-fact. He did not have to mention that he had told Ben's parents all about Charcoal. Ben knew. 'They had a long drive, you know, and they both look very tired, Ben. Now then, tell me what you want me to do.'

The milking was much easier with McGlosker's help, and with a dog that seemed to know exactly what was required of him. The cows came up willingly, even though they were being milked a little early, and eyed Charcoal guardedly all the time. McGlosker turned to Ben once, when Charcoal swung Bossy aside to prevent her making a rush at the gate. The boy knew that he was about to praise the dog's performance, so he scowled, and McGlosker bent his head again to connect one of the suction cups. The milking went on, very efficiently and very quietly. I know what I'll do, Ben thought. I'm not going to let them send Charcoal away.

As soon as they had finished, McGlosker said goodbye. 'I'd better get back, Ben, I've got some work to do at home before it gets dark. Tell your dad that I'll come over again to help in the morning. You've done a sterling job here, Ben, but it's time for you to get back to school now.' He hesitated. 'Your parents look tired.'

He had said it before. Why did he repeat it, like a warning almost? McGlosker seemed reluctant to leave. Ben looked at him stonily, waiting for him to go. 'They look tired,' the man repeated. 'In fact, your mother's exhausted. They've been through a bad time.'

Ben nodded. 'Goodbye, Mr McGlosker,' he said.

And then, because he would not be seeing the man ever again, he added politely, 'And thank you very much for helping.'

When McGlosker had gone, Ben walked back to the house, conscious now of a tight fist of anger bunched inside him. His parents were waiting on the verandah, and his father stooped to welcome Charcoal as the dog approached him, tail wagging.

'We thought we'd say hello to your new friend,' he said, and when Ben remained silent, he tried again. 'What's his name?'

'Charcoal.'

'One of the Emu Creek sheepdogs?'

'Yes.'

His mother was sitting on the step, and as she put her arm around Charcoal the dog leaned against her trustingly. She looked troubled, and yes, Ben thought, McGlosker was right, she did look exhausted. Ben switched his glance away from her.

'You want to buy him,' she said. 'Oh, Ben, I do wish that we could help you, but we just don't have enough money for something like that, especially at this time of the year.'

'I know. It doesn't matter.'

It didn't matter anymore, because he and Charcoal would not be here much longer anyway. Instead of looking pleased that he had accepted the situation so readily, they looked even more troubled.

'Dinner's ready, Ben,' his mother said, after an awkward pause. 'Perhaps we'd all better have an early night so that we can make sure that you catch the bus tomorrow and get to school.'

As Ben passed him in the doorway, his father dropped a hand on his shoulder. 'Thank you, son,' he said. 'You've been wonderful.' Ben moved on, leaving his father's hand dangling.

'I'll take Charcoal for a walk after dinner,' Ben said.

He did not notice what food his mother heaped on his plate, but he made sure that he ate everything, even though he was not hungry. He knew that it might be some time before he had another good meal. He would have to take some of the vet's pellets for Charcoal; enough to tide him over until Ben could buy him some more. And his bankbook, of course; he must take that. He had plenty of money in the bank, not a thousand dollars, but enough for what he needed now. As soon as they had finished eating he walked into his bedroom, collected the bankbook and his coat, and hid a plastic bag in the pocket; he would fill that with the pellets on the way out and no one would notice.

'I'll take Charcoal for that walk now,' he told them both, careful not to say 'goodbye' in case he accidentally made the word sound too significant. This way he could go quietly, without any fuss.

He knew exactly how everything was to be done. Trevor, one of the oldest kids in his class at school, had hitchhiked to Sydney last year. And he had told them all, later, how easy it had been. There had been no trouble getting a lift, he said, because the truck drivers picked you up on the road—most of them liked company while they were driving. If Trevor had been able to do it, so could he. Charcoal would be no bother; even if he was not yet fully recovered, he would be resting in the truck. And when they reached the city, they could go and stay with his grandfather, couldn't they? His hand was already on the doorknob when his father spoke.

'Before you go,' he suggested, rather diffidently, 'perhaps it might be a good time to ring Emu Creek.' And, when Ben nodded, indifferent, he added, 'Do you want to speak to them, or shall I?'

'Suit yourself,' Ben shrugged.

His father was still looking at him, and eventually Ben had to meet his eye. 'Perhaps you should,' his father said. 'There will probably be questions. But, if you like, I'll get the number and give him a general outline of what happened first.'

Ben nodded, fingering the bankbook in his pocket, anxious to be gone. He noted that his father had been prepared for the call, for he was consulting figures on a slip of paper set before him on the table, and dialling them with his good hand. After a few crisp, explanatory sentences his father handed Ben the phone. He lifted it to his ear.

'Hullo.'

The voice on the phone sounded anxious, and upset, and Ben felt a little cheered, for evidently someone else cared about Charcoal. He explained how the crate had fallen from the truck, and what he had done about it. Since he had told McGlosker the story, it had compressed and tightened in his mind so that now it flowed more easily — but more flatly. He was telling it to his parents too, because they were both standing there, listening.

'The driver was going too fast,' he said. Why not tell the whole truth? Then, in answer to a question. 'No, the driver didn't come back for the dog until the next day.' Well, thought Ben, I might save other dogs from being neglected and left untended without water. And, even though the voice on the phone sounded very concerned, he had chosen that mode of transport for Charcoal, hadn't he?

'Will he be all right with you until tomorrow?' the voice asked, still anxious.

'Quite all right,' Ben assured him. They would be in the city by tomorrow, he and Charcoal. He set the phone down. He did not look at his parents. When he reached the verandah, he shovelled some of the pellets quickly into the plastic bag, then they were on their way.

They walked up the drive towards the road. The moon was full, so Ben could see clearly. He had already decided that they would walk along the road in the direction of the junction where it would be easier to pick up a lift because there was more traffic. Ben looked down at Charcoal, checking that the dog was walking easily. He should be able to manage the walk to the junction if they went reasonably slowly and had plenty of rests along the way. Anyway, he could carry him. He had carried him once before.

One thousand dollars. You never had enough money for what you really wanted. No matter how he saved his pocket money, he would never save that much. If he'd been left alone, Charcoal could have stayed with him, and no one need have known, not ever. What did it matter about the insurance, anyway? It was always money. Look what'd happened to Julie, when she tried to buy the horse. Adults were always interfering, making rules to suit themselves.

His parents would not miss him for a while, he was sure. In fact, they had looked so tired that they would probably go straight to bed, and not wait for him to return. They looked tired. McGlosker had not only noticed it, but he had mentioned it twice. Why? It struck Ben as odd now, as it had then, that he should have done so. He remembered the insistent way that McGlosker had said it, as though the words had a special message for Ben.

While he had been thinking, he had slowed right down and stopped, so now he started again, making for the gate. He remembered how he had come this far with his parents when they had set out for the hospital, and how awkwardly and jerkily his mother had driven that afternoon, not smoothly as she usually did. She had been distressed, and frightened. They would not miss him for a while anyway, perhaps not until morning. His mother would go to call him for breakfast, thinking that he had slept late, and then they would find that he had gone. They would be upset.

He found that he had halted again, and he wondered – as he often had recently – why he could not discipline his mind to consider one thing only at a time? Why should it be now that he had to rummage in the cupboard of his memory and drag out that recollection of Julie, talking about her experience on the night of the flood, and when she returned?

'The worst thing about it all,' she told Ben, 'the very worst thing was when I came back, and I saw how exhausted Mum and Dad looked. And I realised that it was all my fault.'

Ben had listened to her then, hardly registering the remark at the time. He had been far more interested in her description of the way the old barn had collapsed, and the flood. Now he stood with his hand on the front gate, all ready to leave, but held still by the chains of Julie's and McGlosker's voices jangling and clinking in his head.

When at last he turned to walk back towards the farmhouse, with Charcoal still padding quietly beside him, he saw that his parents had left the front door open for him, so that the light from the hall shone like a beacon on to the verandah. He sat there for a while with Charcoal, but out of the range of the light, because he knew that he and Charcoal were saying goodbye to each other, and he could not see the dog as clearly, out of the light. After a time, he felt the dog shiver as he was stroking him. It was only a tremor, but Ben was afraid that he might get cold. He rose and went inside.

'Can Charcoal sleep inside tonight?' he asked his mother. She was making a cup of cocoa for him, and he wished that she had not bothered, because he had not even helped her with the dishes after dinner.

'We knew that you'd like to have him inside,' she said. 'Dad's found some clean hessian and he's put that in your room, in the corner. We didn't think that Charcoal was well enough yet to sleep outside.'

'You'll have time together tomorrow, after school,' his father assured him. Ben was ashamed to see how anxious he looked. 'No one will be able to get here from Emu Creek until fairly late in the day; it's a long way.'

Time after school, Ben thought, if I'm lucky – just a couple of hours. But he drank the cocoa, all the same.

The next day seemed to develop a momentum of its own that gathered Ben up with it, and rolled him along. McGlosker arrived early, to help with the milking. He looked pleased – and relieved – to see Ben sitting at the breakfast table. Had he guessed? the boy wondered.

'Good morning, Ben,' was all that McGlosker said, however.

Charcoal chased Ben's bike all the way up to the front gate, but he turned obediently when Ben ordered him to go back. Half wishing that Charcoal had disobeyed him, the boy stood watching him trot back along the drive. He told himself that he should be pleased that the dog had shown no reluctance, for that was one of the reasons that he was so valuable, wasn't it?

Everything went like clockwork that morning, Ben noted with grim amusement, recalling his frantic efforts on Monday. He had plenty of time to set his bike under cover, and then he spent five minutes waiting for the school bus to arrive. When the bus reached Coonara it was still only three-quarters full, and Ben lifted his bag off the seat that he had been saving for Julie, so that she could sit beside him.

'Are your parents back?' she asked.

He told her about Charcoal, and she listened

intently, grimacing angrily when he described how the dog had been left overnight in the crate. At one point she burst into speech.

'You didn't tell me when I came over yesterday. Why didn't you let me see him then?'

'I was half asleep, and anyway, you were in a hurry, remember? If I'd gone into the whole thing, you'd have missed the bus, well and truly.'

'I'd love to see him, but I can't come over tonight, I've got to go to Jindagery with Mum. But tomorrow I could.'

'He'll be gone by then,' Ben explained. His mouth felt dry as ashes. 'The owner is coming today to pick him up.'

And that would be the end of the whole affair, Ben told himself. After that, he would never know what Charcoal was doing, or whether he was happy. Nothing. A dog couldn't write to you, or ring you up and talk to you, even if he was your friend. He'd be gone. Ben tried to listen to what the other kids in the bus were telling him about the new school, but he missed a lot of it. After a while he turned to stare out the window as the trees whizzed by, recalling the way that Charcoal had licked his face when he'd brought Bossy and Star safely back to him, along the road. His friend Charcoal. And now he'd lost him.

But during that first day at school he was ashamed to find that he almost forgot Charcoal at times, because he had so much to learn and so much to remember: teachers' names, classrooms, books, and new faces. The day was so crowded and passed so quickly that he was quite shocked when he glanced at his watch in the afternoon and realised that he would soon be catching the bus back home.

It left on time. Julie, heading down to Jindagery with her mother, did not catch the bus, so Ben sat quietly by himself, too tense and anxious to talk to the others. He checked his watch every few minutes, wondering why they'd put the slowest of the buses on his route. How long would he and Charcoal have together before the man from Emu Creek arrived? Probably no more than an hour or two, but they could spend whatever time they had down by the river, and up on Mount Everest. He had not had time to take Charcoal up there before. Perhaps Charcoal would remember Ben and the farm, even when he was living somewhere else.

He watched the kids who lived in Coonara get off at their stop. It won't be long now, he thought, and I'll get my bike and race home on it. I don't want to waste any time. But when he reached his stop and got out, he heard a car horn. Insistent. He looked around to see McGlosker sitting in his utility, beckoning him urgently.

'Hop in, Ben,' he called. 'I've got your bike on the back.'

He hardly waited for Ben to get settled in the utility before he was racing down the highway. The boy sat with his hands pressed hard together. Something was wrong. He was afraid to ask.

'I thought this'd be the quickest way to get you home,' McGlosker told him. 'The man from Emu Creek is here already – he came earlier than we thought – he took a plane to Jindagery, then a hire car across. Your dad asked me if I'd pick you up at the bus stop and rush you home, and I believe your mother's doing her level best to delay the fellow with afternoon tea.'

He swung in to Ben's farm through a gate already opened for them, raced down the drive, bumped over the cattlegrid, and almost skidded to a halt.

'He's still here,' he said, indicating the large station wagon.

But Ben could see that the stranger was ready to leave. He was standing, talking with Ben's parents beside the car, and Charcoal was already inside, lying along the back seat. I can't even touch him again, the boy thought forlornly, but McGlosker leaned across and pulled the door open.

'There you are,' he said to Ben. And then to the stranger, 'I know that Ben'll want to say goodbye to the dog.'

The man nodded, and Ben noticed that he had kind eyes. But it was too hard to say anything in front of everyone, so after a moment he stood back and closed the door again. At least, he thought, Charcoal's not going back in that awful truck.

'I've been hearing what you did for Charcoal, and I can't thank you enough, Ben,' the owner said. 'I'm taking him home with me to have him checked out by my vet, to make sure that he's one hundred per cent fit. And when I send him to his new owner, I'm sending him by air.' He shook his head, his smile gone. 'I won't be using that carrier again. The fellow who used to arrange all my transport retired, and his replacement turned out to be a swindler. I paid him for plane or rail travel for my dogs, and he subcontracted to any rogue who could drive a truck apparently, and pocketed the difference.'

He stopped for a moment, and shook hands with Ben gravely. The boy could not help liking him, even though he was taking Charcoal away.

'I don't know how long he'd have got away with his scheme,' the man continued, 'and if it hadn't been for you, Ben, other dogs would have suffered, too. The man was running a real racket – it wasn't just me and my dogs – evidently he's been defrauding a lot of other people too, the police tell me. He'll be charged.'

Apparently he had offered Ben's parents some

money to compensate them, for he continued, 'I wish I could have persuaded your parents to take something, Ben, for all the trouble that this's caused you.'

Ben cringed inside, then relaxed again as his father replied firmly, 'No. Our son loved the dog. He was glad to help him.'

'Well, I guess we'd better be on our way,' the man said, and to Ben, 'thank you again for all you did.'

'Ben! There's a letter for you.'

For him? He took it from his father reluctantly. The heat of their old tin letterbox had dried out the paper so that it crackled when he folded it over to put in his pocket.

'Aren't you going to read it?'

Ben shook his head. His father stood waiting uncertainly, then he turned away.

'I'll read it later,' Ben called after him.

He strolled very slowly up to the dam, and stood there for a while in the sunshine. His presence disturbed the small family of ducks so that they fussed rapidly across the water to the far side where they stayed in a little bunch, watchful. He sat down at the water's edge, feeling the letter rustle dryly as he moved. It was two weeks since Charcoal had gone, and he knew that the letter was from Emu Creek. He had recognised the little emu motif on the edge of the envelope, and his father must have seen it too.

He supposed that he would have to read it eventually, but he knew already what it would contain. Thank you for saving Charcoal. The man had said it before, but he probably thought that he should write. Perhaps, news about Charcoal — where he was, and the work that he was doing now. Ben did not want to know where Charcoal had been sent. He simply did not want to know. Abstractedly, he drew lines in the soft wet earth at the dam's edge, then stopped abruptly because he saw that he had drawn a rectangular box. He wished now that he had never seen Charcoal, and that the crate had not fallen where it had.

But, before he could prevent them, his thoughts hurried along a little dark arcade. What if it had fallen at some other spot, and never been found? He jumped to his feet to escape the horrible thought of Charcoal in the box, whimpering unheard.

He walked towards Mount Everest, shoulders well back and hands in his pockets, feeling the letter rustling there. He whistled. Sounds carried, and if his parents could see him and hear him, they would know that he was happy. He did not want to go back to the house until he had read the letter, and Mount Everest was the furthest that he could go. It did not seem nearly as steep today, and he supposed that it was because he was getting older.

When he reached the top he stood gazing across the hills. He had forgotten that the grass grew so thickly, here at the top. It was the first time that he had climbed Mount Everest since the day of the truck, and now he wished that he had stayed down by the dam. He could have read the letter just as easily there.

It was very still, and the sun felt warm on his back. Sounds floated gently around him in the clear air. He heard the door of one of the sheds creak as his father pulled it wide open, and he saw his mother walking across the garden with a basket full of apples from the tree. He heard one of McGlosker's dogs barking on the hill opposite.

He knew that he could not put off reading the letter any longer, so he took it out of his pocket and weighed it in his hand. What if he simply tore it up here, and scattered it? His hand tightened, and then relaxed. No, that would do no good at all, and his parents would want to know what was in the letter anyway.

He opened it very, very slowly to delay the moment further, slitting the envelope carefully along the top. He drew out three sheets of paper, each printed at the top corner with the now familiar 'Emu Creek'. Three sheets. Why would they need three sheets of paper? 'Dear Ben,' he read. 'I know that you will be pleased to hear that Charcoal has recovered very well, and now shows few signs of his accident.'

Ben stopped reading, for he knew what was coming. Since Charcoal was better, he would be with his new owner, working the sheep again. Ben tried to focus on a clump of pink heath close to his foot, but his eyes misted over. He scrubbed at them angrily and forced himself to read the rest of the letter. Get it finished, he told himself, and then wipe the whole incident from your life.

'There is a problem, however.' Ben stopped again, squinting at the word. A problem? Yes, it definitely said 'problem'. His heart began to hammer. Bad news was coming. He read on as fast as he could.

'Because of the accident that the dog suffered, the vet cannot guarantee that Charcoal might not develop weaknesses during the later part of his working life, and we are too proud of our reputation here to risk that happening. I have a favour to ask, therefore . . .'

Ben was having trouble reading the thick spreading writing; it did not seem to be making sense because it was all out of step with the words that he had expected and had already composed in his head. He searched for the top of the second page, and found it. ' . . . which you will want to discuss with your parents. I know that you do not have a dog, Ben, so I wonder if you might like to keep Charcoal at your farm, especially since your father indicated to me that the dog had been of some help to you, and that you had grown fond of him. There would be no charge, of course,' Ben checked these words again; he was bewildered, 'since you would be helping us over the difficulty of finding a good, and suitable home for him now.'

Ben had to turn over to the third page, but his hands were now shaking so much that he dropped the letter, and he had to pick it up and scrabble the pages around until he found the final paragraph. It was a short one. 'Could you, or your parents, ring me as soon as possible, to let me know what you decide.'

Ben turned back to the beginning and read the letter again. Then, to check that there was no mistake, he read it all once more, this time aloud. No charge. Those two words were beautifully clear, so it must be right. No charge. He must tell his mother and father at once. They must ring at once. He was scrambling down Mount Everest, shouting, the letter clutched tight.

'Mum! Dad!' he yelled.

He startled the ducks again as he raced past the dam, but this time he did not notice. He could see his mother in the distance, standing still, her face upraised, questioning. His father was nearer. He looked up, and then began to run to meet him. Ben wondered why his father was laughing, until he realised that he, himself, was laughing, and crying, and waving the letter as he ran.

'It's Charcoal!' he cried, even before they were close enough to understand, but he wanted to say it over and over, to make sure that it was true. 'It's Charcoal! He's coming home!'